WE

JOHN DICKINSON

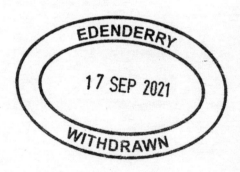

David Fickling Books

OXFORD · NEW YORK

31 Beaumont Street
Oxford OXI 2NP, UK

WE

A DAVID FICKLING BOOK 978 0 385 61789 5

Published in Great Britain by David Fickling Books,
a division of Random House Children's Books
A Random House Group Company

This edition published 2010

3 5 7 9 10 8 6 4 2

Mixed Sources
Product group from well-managed
forests and other controlled sources
www.fsc.org Cert no. TT-COC-2139
© 1996 Forest Stewardship Council
FSC

Set in Adobe Garamond

DAVID FICKLING BOOKS
31 Beaumont Street, Oxford, OX1 2NP

www.kidsatrandomhouse.co.uk
www.rbooks.co.uk

Addresses for companies within The Random House Group Limited can be found at:
www.randomhouse.co.uk/offices.htm

THE RANDOM HOUSE GROUP Limited Reg. No. 954009

A CIP catalogue record for this book is available from the British Library.

Printed and bound in Great Britain by Clays Ltd, St Ives plc

I

He had asked to be alone when he woke. After all, he had reasoned, from now on he would always be alone.

They had told him there would be no pain from the operation. He had looked up the techniques they would use, checked the possible complications and had understood why they had said that. Nevertheless, something in him was surprised to discover that they had been right. There was none. There was only emptiness.

He blinked, automatically holding his eyelids closed for just that fraction of a second that would summon his displays. But no voice spoke in his head. No images appeared, no lists, nothing.

There were no weather reports, news pictures, financial statements, alerts concerning the state of his house or vehicle or the transmission systems that he was supposed to maintain. There were no demands from his supervisors. And there were no personal messages. Like everyone else he always went to those first. But there were none – no loving images, no jokes or pictures, no one wishing him luck or promising to remember him. There was nothing more from Her. There never would be.

His fingers felt gingerly for his eyes. The artificial lenses were gone. He touched the soft hollow behind his right ear. There was a small dressing there. It was numb when he pressed at it. The wound it covered would be tiny. There was no pain. But the implanted systems he had carried all his adult life had been taken away. Of course they had been. That was what it was all about.

He focused on the things he could see.

He was lying in a bed, looking up at a white ceiling. The room was unfamiliar. Automatically he blinked again, summoning the answers to his questions. But the displays did not respond.

That moment – that first question, when his eyes blinked, his mind listened and waited for the displays, and *nothing* came – was the most dreadful he had ever known. It was as if he had suddenly put a foot out over the edge of a cliff and felt the depth beneath his toes. His ears heard a sound – a strangled gasp. His own throat had made it.

Now his brain lumbered into action (brushing aside the habits of thought that said to him, *Consult! Consult!*). He did know why he was here. He knew where 'here' was. It was a room adjoining the implants surgery. He had been left here to recover. He had expected that. He had been put to sleep during the operation, to protect his mind from the moment of removal from the networks. Now he had woken. He was alone because he had asked that he should be.

How long had he been asleep?

What was the time?

Automatically he blinked again. But there was only deadness. Nothing lit in his brain to tell him what the time was.

Again, that lurch in his stomach – that moment of nightmare! *What is the time?* No answer.

Sunlight came in through the window. It was day. But what time was it?

Which day was it?

He drew a long breath. It shook in his throat.

He had been removed from the networks. There had been good operational reasons. There was a job to do, a long distance away. The networks did not work there. So he must be without them. He had known that.

But he had not known it would be like *this*!

Think. Breathe. Do not try to consult.

Use the senses.

He looked around him. His sight, once he had stopped hunting for projected look-up displays, worked perfectly well. He saw the calm pale browns of the bedclothes. He saw the single table by his bed, the cabinet in which his clothes hung, the old-fashioned, inactive walls. Opposite him there was a large mirror. It showed a man lying on a bed, propped on one elbow, looking back at him. It was himself.

His face was the same: the light, even pigment of his skin, the round cheeks and the sloping forehead framed in fair hair so short that his head seemed like a block set upon his muscular shoulders. He looked healthy. Nothing in his appearance had changed. Except the way the eyes stared, as if they were afraid.

Again he looked around. Things that yesterday would have been a background to his displays were real and immediate now. They were like soft punches on his brain: the white ceiling, the white walls, the window showing sky; the brown cabinet, brown bedclothes. The eyes of the man in the mirror.

And again. White ceiling, white walls . . .

Why white? he wondered.

He blinked. Nothing answered. Grumbling with the unusual effort, his thoughts stirred.

White reflects light. The more white there was in the room, the more light there would be. The more light there was, the less need to provide artificial lighting.

It was not his field but the idea seemed sound. And it had not taken him very much longer to reach it in his own mind than it would have done to look it up on the networks. Good.

But . . .

It was only an idea. It was the product of one brain, working alone. It should be put for confirmation – especially since light and colour were not in his professional field. And . . .

And it could not be put for confirmation.

The thought must stay in his head. Because he had been removed from the networks, it could not go to anyone else. It would for ever be useless to anyone but him. He would never know whether it was accurate or not.

This was another bad moment. Again it was one he had foreseen, and again he had not foreseen how much it would hurt that his ideas had nowhere to go.

Of course it did not matter that his theory about the white walls and ceiling could not be shared. Such a simple thought would have been available to everyone on any network since the very beginning. But the same would be true for any insight he might have in his professional field. All his skills – all his understanding of the physics and engineering of radio telemetry – were now blocked off from the rest of humanity. Others would be trained to take his place. In training and operating they might use data that he had laid in the networks. But from now on he could make no contribution. He was useless. Except for the one overriding purpose for which he was being prepared, he was useless to everyone living now or in the future.

Again he heard a sound – a sound that his own throat had made.

Abruptly he threw off his bedclothes and swung his legs over to the floor. The calm brown flooring was cool beneath his soles.

Look. See. Think.

He repeated it to himself. *Look. See. Think.* He had barely seen anything since waking in this new, empty world.

He rose to his feet. The tops of buildings bobbed into view beyond the window. Carefully (fearing, in some deep part of himself, that his sense of balance might have been robbed from him along with everything else) he made his way across the room. He looked out.

He was high up, which was unusual. The implants surgery occupied a floor in one of the old 'skyscraper' buildings that still dominated the centre of the city. There was another opposite him, currently in the throes of demolition, but enough of it still remained to show what it had been: a tower of dirty tinted glass, rising to many times the height of any modern structure. Yesterday, approaching the surgery, he had noted these improbable buildings that stacked storey on top of storey in so many layers. Had he wished, his eyes could have blinked and tracked a few times and called up the reasons why recent generations had felt it useful to cram their physical bodies so close together. But his thoughts had been on other things. Now, when each sight seemed to be flooding in to fill all the huge spaces that had opened in his mind, he could only stare and wonder at that insane rush for the sky – the bewildering product of another time.

And he would not form any theories. There was no point, if they could be neither confirmed nor shared.

He looked down at the city. He saw the lines and lines of trees, planted along the verges of the avenues. He saw the angular shapes of old but still habitable buildings, constructed from masonry, peeping from among the green. Further off, the trees seemed to thicken and the glimpses of buildings showed not the old straight lines of tiled roofs and brick walls but the subtle curves of modern bubble-houses gleaming in the sun. There was the bright curl of the river, the beautiful inverted arcs of the old suspension bridges and the less pleasing but more functional criss-cross of modern cables that carried whatever traffic needed to pass from one bank to the other these days.

No sound could be heard from up here, behind the glass of the window. And there was not much movement to be seen. The occasional vehicle or walker was passing peacefully down the huge avenues that previous city-dwellers had thought necessary to carry their transport. Yet all that landscape was humming with life, with messages passing from person to person, invisibly, inaudibly, but all the time. The city was a great living thing. And none of it was for him. None of it could reach him.

All that living – and none of it could touch him! He could no more feel them than he could hear or see them, up here. That . . . That was what was different now. It always would be.

His fist thumped the window, gently, but enough to make it shake and for him to feel the impact afterwards. He wondered why he had done it. He looked at his hand and found he could no longer see it clearly. His sight had blurred. He wanted to screw up his eyes.

Something was happening to him! He could not see! His eyes were hot. His breathing was coming in gasps that he could not control. Something wet was on his cheeks. It was not sweat – not any kind of sweat that he knew. He could not call for help. He had no way of calling for help! His mind was dumb – dumb, and beginning to fight with panic.

But there was a way. There was the red alarm button by the bedside. When they had showed it to him, he had noted it but had never thought that he might use such a thing. Now he must try, before things got worse. He stumbled back to the bedside. He fumbled for the button and pressed it clumsily with the tip of his finger. Then he sat on the bed, not daring to move. He felt the fit subsiding. His breathing was more even now. He wiped his cheeks on his arm. His sight returned, although his eyes still stung. He tried to order his mind. He tried to remember the various possible complications that could arise from his operation and match them with the symptoms he was experiencing. He could not. He longed desperately to be back on the networks, just for a few moments, so that he would be able to look them up and know what was happening to him. Knowing was so important. Not knowing was horrible – not knowing, when he should have been able to know! And no one was coming to help him. He had pressed the alarm and they were not coming! How long ago had he pressed it?

Again he could not know.

They came. Two people entered the room. He recognized one, a gentle-faced man in blue surgical overalls who had informed him beforehand of the likely course of the operation. The other was a young woman with short brown hair about whom he knew nothing.

Yesterday he would have known. Yesterday, even before she had stepped into his sight, he would have known her age, qualifications, family status and preferred protocols. Notes of her financial status, social and antisocial behaviours (if any) would have been available. He could have dealt with her with confidence, knowing she knew the same about him. Now he was helpless.

The doctor's eyes blinked and tracked. The woman spoke.

'You pressed the alarm?' she said.

She was a Talker: someone who was trained to use her throat and mouth to form words so that it was possible to communicate with individuals who, for whatever reason, were not on the networks. She was a Talker for the doctor.

He looked at the doctor. The mild, concerned face looked back at him.

No, not at him. The eyes were not focused on him. They were following their displays. If they saw his physical body at all, it was through a veil of images and symbols, options, communications with the Talker, all marshalled to address whatever the problem might be.

And then he realized that he could not tell them what it was.

It should have been so easy. An image of his own face, taken from his handcam and focusing on the symptoms. Colours of red and amber to convey alarm. Perhaps a word or two – *dangerous side-effect query*. Quick and unambiguous – that was all a message needed to be. And he could not do it. He had no handcam to take images, no display and pupil tracker with which to transmit, no World Ear with which to receive. Everything was gone.

To communicate now, he had to talk. He could not do that either. He knew what words should sound like but he had had no practice forming them. Not for years and years.

'Are you well?' said the Talker. Her voice had a gentle sound.

He opened his mouth.

'Aa . . . Aaah . . .' It was all he could manage.

And in his stress his symptoms were worsening again. His eyes were hot and screwed up. His cheeks were wet. He choked.

Desperately he jabbed his fingers at his face, pointing. '*Aaarh!*' he said.

The doctor's eyes focused. He bent to look closely. His face wore the detached concern of one who knew he would never suffer as the person before him was suffering. His pupils tracked.

'It is Tears,' translated the Talker. 'Just Tears. They are . . .'

She hesitated. The information the doctor was giving her had far outpaced her ability to put it into speech.

'They are normal,' she said.

It was not a good choice of word. Tears were not normal. None of them could remember crying. But it was the best she could do.

II

That first stage – the operation, together with subsequent therapies and speech training – took knowledge, the right tools and materials, and some man-days of time from a number of specialists.

The next required an effort greater than the output of a hundred thousand human lifetimes.

At a moment determined by the relative positions of planets and the Sun, his training was interrupted. He was taken to another surgery, one that specialized in anaesthetics, and there he was put into a sleep. His body was fitted into a dynamic harness capable of exercising his limbs gently while his mind was unconscious. Then he and his harness were slung in a capsule and taken to a place unlike any other in the world.

The vehicle that carried him left the city and passed through rich green countryside speckled with gardens and the shining domes of houses. It climbed through hills that were covered with thick forests teeming with birds, insects and brightly coloured life. Hundreds of different species crammed every square metre here, shrieking, scuttling, growing, decaying, but he saw none of it. He did not see the great blue gem of the sea, flecked with white, when it rose into view as the road climbed. Nor did he see the dusty uplands, coated with low thorns, across which his vehicle sped for hours under a deep blue sky.

And then in the sky there was a line.

It was like a crack in the blue, a pencil-stroke drawn from the heavens straight down to the earth. The vehicle sped on towards it, spurring light dust-clouds in its wake, and for a long time nothing changed. There was only the earth, the sky and that straight, impossible line that grew neither thicker nor nearer.

In the last stage of the approach the road snaked among low, rocky rises. As it snaked, a watcher from the vehicle would have seen the line appear to move against the thorn-covered hills beyond it. Only then could a human eye have been sure that it was something that really existed. The line was now just a few kilometres away, rising in a steep curve from the ground. It rose and rose. A bend in the road revealed the buildings and other structures that clustered at its foot. By now a traveller in the vehicle would have had to crane backwards for his eye to follow it up. And at last it would have gained a width that the mind could have grasped. It was a cable, as thick as the trunk of an ancient tree, yet in comparison to its length far more slender and frail than a spider's thread, rising from the Earth to the sky.

The passenger saw none of this. He was asleep. And the people who accompanied him and received him did not see it either. They moved with the live displays flickering across their vision and barely glanced up at the thing that soared and disappeared above their heads.

The cable was made of special carbon-based materials designed for this one purpose: to create a structure strong enough to reach into space without collapsing under its own weight. It was nearly forty thousand kilometres long – almost as long as the imaginary line of the equator itself. Its far end was anchored to a satellite in geostationary orbit. And there it hung, like some line of longitude come adrift from Earth: a ladder that men had built towards the stars.

Clutching at its base, in a cocoon of red gantries, was a man-made insect the size of a small house. It was white, sprouting black solar panels like wings. But it was blind. It had no windows because it had no crew. Its operations were all automatic or controlled from the ground. It sat with its nose pointed up the first gentle curve of the cable, waiting for the man who lay unconscious in his capsule.

The precious burden was lifted up the gantries and placed inside the giant white insect. Then more checks were performed: on the occupant; on the capsule with its life-supporting array of instruments and its reservoirs of supplies; and on the cable-vehicle itself, which had to pass a hundred routine tests before the start of each climb.

Waiting. Results. Orders. A risk was noted. Permission was sought for a ten-day postponement.

Permission was denied. The astronomical window was too small for any delay. The risk must be accepted.

More orders. Codes were entered. Systems aboard the white insect woke. Gantries were withdrawn. The black wings trained themselves to the Sun. A gentle humming filled the site.

More waiting.

Then a signal, sent automatically from the white insect to its controllers. *Ready.*

More codes were entered and acknowledged. The final one was repeated three times for confirmation.

The hum deepened and increased. Gently the white insect began to rise along the cable, curving away upwards from the ground. Clinging to the impossible thread, it needed nothing like the acceleration required by rockets of past eras. The force of the Earth pulled on it but could not slow it. The detail of the launching site was lost in the enormous green-brown of the diminishing land. Up and up the insect sped, like a train hurrying into the sky. The solar panels angled to catch the Sun. The Earth turned but the cable turned with it, towed by the satellite at the far end. It turned four times on its axis. And still the insect hurried up and up and up out of the little, safe well of gravity that life inhabited, out to the rim of space.

On the last stage of its journey it slowed. Here, one-tenth of the distance between the Earth and the Moon, the anchoring satellite swung at the end of its line. It was almost a little moon itself, a near-Earth asteroid diverted to its current orbit, so that the cable's outer end would be secured while the white insects scuttled to and fro. It had huge solar panels, and directional rockets to permit slight variations to its orbit should drifting debris threaten either it or the precious cable. It was Earth's outer door to space.

It was also its shipyard. Here, crews of remotely controlled robots moved along runners to assemble spacecraft that would have no need to fight their way up from the pit of Earth's gravity. Along one gantry lay the skeleton of a craft five hundred metres long, the first of a non-recoverable fleet planned for the hundred-year project to make a habitable world from the hell of Venus. The robots slid patiently to and fro along their scaffolding, bearing components to the vessel, adding to it bit by bit like metal ants feeding a huge queen.

Out here, beyond the atmosphere, there was no sound at all. But there was still vibration, dropping in pitch as the cable-vehicle slowed and slowed to dock at the inbound gantry. Then there was a pause. At workstations forty thousand kilometres away on Earth, routine checks were performed.

Satisfactory.

Commands were transmitted to the station. A hatch on the insect opened. Great arms reached down into it and fastened around the capsule inside.

More checks. Secure.

The arms lifted the capsule with its living, sleeping burden out of the cable-craft. Silently, passionlessly, they bore it along a gantry to a smaller spacecraft which had completed its assembly and tests some weeks before. This craft had two huge arms, folded in three sections along the gantry. At the end of each arm was a large globe. In one of these globes a hatch opened, revealing a small chamber surrounded by massive shielding. The capsule was placed inside. The hatch closed.

Six hours passed. After more checks and conferences on Earth, final commands were given. Gently the spacecraft separated from the satellite and began its journey. At a safe distance the two arms unfolded. Locked in their extended position, they were each a kilometre long. Gently they began to turn in a giant cartwheel around the spacecraft, one globe acting as counter-weight to the other, to simulate the effect of a light gravity field pulling on the body in its capsule.

Down on the surface, congratulations rippled around the command centres, universities, engineering concerns and surgeries that had been directly involved. There were images and comments on the news sites and among the wider population. None of it reached the sleeping man, riding in his tiny bubble through the vastness of space.

Six months later there was another wave of interest on Earth, mostly among the space engineering community, as the craft made its passage past the Sun. Anxious eyes monitored the levels of radiation absorbed by the shielding on the passenger globe. Automatic messages from the vessel reported that systems aboard remained normal. The capsule detected no apparent damage to its occupant. At the closest point the rockets fired to kick the little spaceship onward. Swung by the enormous gravity of the star, it accelerated away into the void.

There were more congratulations. Then interest faded as effort was switched to other things. But it did not die altogether. A rota of staff checked the regular reports that came back from the craft and the capsule within it, day in, day out. Occasional corrections were discussed and trans-mitted. So Earth settled down to watch as the tiny artificial mote diminished and diminished towards the outer edge of the solar system.

It watched, patiently, for eight years.

III

Sleep held him close, like a membrane around a new-born thing. He was blind with it. He stirred feebly but it held him. In his darkness he could hear a voice saying something. It was a woman's voice.

There was something strange about the words. They were like nothing he had heard in his training classes. They were drawn out, and some of them changed in pitch as they were uttered. There was music in them. Of course he remembered music. There had been days when he had set it to run through his head continuously. He had not heard it made from a human throat before, because there were better and easier ways of doing it. But he knew it was possible. There was a word for it.

The woman was 'singing'.

Was this a dream? He had not had a dream in so long. He could not remember how long. All this long sleep had been a blackness. He could barely imagine the other side of it.

He was lying on something solid. He thought that there should have been a harness round him but there was not. If there ever had been one, it was gone.

If he was asleep, he was not sure that he wanted to wake. He thought that if he did he might be sick. There was something wrong with his head, as if there was too much fluid in it. There was something wrong in his throat too. He could not breathe through his nose.

The singing had stopped. He heard a movement.

'Are you awake yet?' said the woman's voice.

After a moment he felt a touch on his wrist. Fingers that were not his covered his pulse. They were warm. He did not think this could be a dream.

'Oh, come on! Wake up and talk to me,' said the voice. 'I'm getting nervous!'

His hand was put gently back where it had been lying. He heard her move away. There was an irregular clicking sound. He did not recognize it. He would not have dreamed of sounds he did not recognize.

The singing began again. He would not have dreamed that either.

He opened his eyes.

The first thing he saw was a bright surface curving over his head. The light it emitted rippled with little wavelets of orange. He knew exactly what it was. It was the wall of a modern bubble-chamber: active, so that occupants could set it to project whatever images, colours and light-levels they chose. He had not thought there would be one out here.

Out here, meaning . . .

He lifted his head.

The chamber was small. There was just room in it for the bed on which he lay, for the workstation and for the woman who sat there, humming as her fingers played up and down on a peculiar array of mechanical keys.

He looked at the woman. And he knew at once that he was indeed *out here*.

It was as if some child had drawn her. Her proportions were all wrong. Her head was big, her face puffy and swollen. Her skin was so pale that it was almost white. Her body was shapeless in her dark overalls. Her arms and legs and neck were dreadfully thin. There seemed to be no muscle on them. They could be little more than bone, so delicate that they could not possibly carry her. She was like a giant mantis, distorted and horrible to look at.

But she did not seem to be suffering in her condition. She sat poised at her workstation with her delicate fingers nibbling at the mechanical keyboard and her eyes on figures that danced on a wall-screen before her. She was frowning as she worked, as if she was having to think about what she was doing and did not really enjoy this kind of mental activity.

There was a rich, ruddy sheen to her hair, which was tied back from her face. And when she looked round at him, her pony-tail floated as if she were suspended in water. She saw him watching her.

'Hey, that's better!' she said. Her voice was light, clipped and a little dry. 'I was beginning to worry. How do you feel?'

He had to think about it.

His head ached. There seemed to be something wrong with his throat. His nose was blocked. He felt sick. And of course he was weak – weaker than he had ever been in his life.

Experimentally, he sat up. Despite his own frailty his body seemed to flow upwards from the couch. The blanket that had been over him slipped away and drifted gently to the floor, rippling slowly as it fell.

Gravity here was less than one-tenth of that on Earth.

He looked down at himself. He saw that he was naked. And his body was not his any more.

He was looking at limbs that were as spindly as hers. The great muscles of calf and thigh had wasted almost to nothing. All the meat of them had gone. The knees stood out like knobbly balls at the joints of sticks. His arms sprouted from the corners of his undiminished torso, look-ing feeble and ridiculous. If he had not recognized a small mole, clinging obstinately in the crook of his elbow, he

26

would have thought they belonged to someone else. Gingerly he lifted one arm and flexed it. Only the smallest, pathetic bulging showed where his biceps had been. His skin was dead white. No sun had touched it for eight years.

And for eight years, while he had slept, his body had been exposed to a programme of artificial gravity and exercise designed to adapt him for his existence here. His mass had reduced. His muscles had wasted. The calcium in his bones had diminished, leaving them feeble and brittle. If he stood on the Earth now he would collapse at once. His skeleton would splinter under his weight. He would lie in agony, helpless as a stranded jellyfish. Here . . .

He was like her, as deformed as she was.

He looked at himself – at the limbs that might have belonged to someone else. And he felt a kind of horror, but so dimly and quietly that this too might have been the horror of someone else. Memory tapped from the far side of his long, black sleep, telling him that there had been a time when he had known that this would happen to him. He had known and accepted the changes that were coming. There was no need for weight-bearing muscles now. There never would be. And from now on the fluids in his body would always rise to his head, blocking his nose and making his face puffy like hers. He would live for the rest of his life with this insect's body and a permanent head cold. Because that was how things were, out here.

He said nothing. After a little he frowned and shifted himself along the bed to try the easy gravity. He reached down to pick up the blanket and draw it around his waist. It floated and settled slowly over his bony thighs. The woman rose and stepped towards him. He saw her cross the short distance between them in one flowing skip, seeming to move in slow motion. Her limbs, though frail, carried her easily.

'How do you feel?' she repeated.

He thought about it. Then he said: 'Yes.'

'Yes?' She looked puzzled. 'Do you mean that you feel well?'

He frowned again. She was talking far more quickly than his speech tutors had done, back before his eight-year night. And although he could understand her well enough, he could not hope to speak as she did.

But the answer was easy, after all. Positive feedback. It should be 'Yes' again.

'Yes,' he said.

'Are you sure? How's your sight? Can you see clearly? Or are you getting double vision, for example? Headache? Sickness? What can you tell me?'

He thought. It was an effort, trying to deal in words. But he was going to have to get used to it.

'Yes,' he said. Yes, he could see clearly.

'No,' he said, meaning that he did not have double vision.

And 'Yes,' again. He did have a headache.

Then he stopped, because he saw that she thought something was wrong.

'Can you tell me your name?' she asked.

Name?

He knew what a name was. It was used like a reference number, in speech. Of course it was inferior to a reference number because there was no guarantee that a name would be unique. In any population of a thousand or more, confusion could arise.

But out here, the entire population, including himself, was just four. Names were easier to say than numbers. So here the balance of advantage did favour names.

And of course he had a name. He knew it quite well, even though he could not remember when he had last had to use it.

So he said: 'Yes.'

He saw her face change. For some reason his answer had worried her even more. Why was positive feedback worrying? What was he doing wrong?

He was nervous. Of course he was nervous. It was all difficult. He had known it would be difficult but that did not help. Picking words (so *slow!*), looking at what had happened to his body, trying to adjust to this new place – he knew that he had expected it all, somewhere back in his past. He had been trained for all of it. And yet it was still difficult. Now he was doing something wrong and he couldn't think what it was. Panic was beginning to stir.

She looked more closely at him. He could sense her anxiety even before she spoke.

'Please tell me your name,' she said.

'Mun . . . Munro.' He was not used to saying it. But it came out right the second time.

She let out her breath. Her face cleared. 'That's all right. Though mostly we just use first names here. So I'm May and you're Paul – unless you want us to call you something else. Do you mind being called Paul?'

'No.'

'Paul, then. And you're not confused, are you, Paul? For a moment I thought you must be. But it's just that you're not used to speaking, isn't it?'

'Yes!' he said emphatically.

She laughed. 'Yes, no, yes, no . . . Have they stopped speaking altogether back home? No – don't you answer that,' she added as she saw him beginning to think again. 'I'm supposed to be checking you. That's what we're doing. First tell me – how's the throat? Does it hurt?'

'No.'

'Not painful but a bit stiff perhaps?'

'Yes.'

'No surprise there. Your larynx was all one huge sore when we got you into the station. You've been eight years on ventilation, breathing through a tube down your throat. Even that clever little nozzle you were on was rubbing you to bits by the time you landed. I've kept some images of what the inside of your mouth looked like when I first got you, if you're interested. Now' – she reached down and put fingers that were like pale twigs on his shin – 'could you try standing up for me, Paul? Carefully.'

Obediently, clumsily, he stood. He felt her fingers testing his bone as it took the strain – the light strain of his diminished body in this gentle gravity field.

'Very good!' she said, releasing him.

She took him briskly through the checks. Height: one metre eighty-four (slightly more than on departure). Weight: just under five kilograms, whatever that meant in this gravity. Blood pressure. Eyesight. Reactions.

'Yeah, that's good,' she said. 'Do you need a rest now?'

'No.'

'Sure? You're going to tire quickly, though. So look out for that. All right then. Maybe you could try taking some steps for me?'

He hesitated. Then he leaned forward. It seemed to him that he had to lean much too far and wait too long before he sensed himself beginning to fall and could push off with his foot. He flew.

'Careful!' she cried, catching him with an arm across his chest, so that instead of sailing across the room he spun slowly with her like a dancer and came to rest on his toes.

Her head was close to his. It filled his vision. He saw that it was in fact not quite as horrible as he had first thought when he had seen it so unnaturally balanced on top of her body. Yes, her skin was shockingly pale, her cheeks puffy with fluids, but her face-bones were delicate and her eyes had widened just a little in alarm – alarm for him. And she was small. She had to crane right back to look up at him. His mind jerked back to the woman he had left on Earth, who had held him and looked up at him just like this at their last parting. Who had buried her head on his chest and whose sadness had been pain for them both.

The woman released him.

'Take it carefully, yeah?' she said. 'If you push yourself off like that you'll fly across the room. And your bones are much, much more brittle than they were. You don't want to go smashing into anything. Secret is, don't think about it. Your body should already know how to control itself. That's what it's been learning while you were asleep. Let it do the job for you. Try again – and don't think.'

Pushing aside the memory of that other face, he tried again.

But he couldn't help thinking about control. All his conscious effort was focused on it because he was doing it for the first time. His feet moved him in a long skip, floating through the air to the far wall. It was still too hard! He put out his hand to break the impact and felt the orange-pulsing surface give slightly as he pressed against it.

He paused to steady himself. The wall beneath his hand seemed thicker than any chamber wall on Earth would have been. There would be good reasons for that, he thought.

He turned himself with his hands and took another step back, this time landing on the other foot.

'Hey, better!' said May, clapping. 'You know, I think you're almost perfect! When we got here we were all sick and frail. I'd have hospitalized the lot of us if it had been possible. But there's a lot of cleverness back on Earth. And it's learning all the time. You've been kept doing just the right amount while you were on your way here. Still, no risks, yeah? It's going to be bed and rehab exercises only to begin with. And after I let you go I want you to come and see me every day so I can check on you. We'll keep that up until I think it's safe to stop. And if you start to feel at all uncomfortable, in any way, you must tell me at once. I can't help you if you don't.'

'Yes,' he said.

She raised her eyebrows. 'I'm going to ban you from saying that, Paul. "Yes" and "No" all the time! If you want to say "Yes" or "No" you'll have to say something else as well. If you don't practise, you won't improve. Now, are you ready to meet the others? Just for a short time. We've been jumping up and down to see you – I tell you, when we took you out of that capsule it was like unwrapping the biggest and best birthday present ever! It was very nearly Van's birthday too. Will you be all right to do that?'

He thought about it.

'Yes,' he said.

'Yes . . . ?'

There had to be other words, she had said. Of course she had been joking. But she was right.

'Yes, May,' he said. She smiled again. And he was pleased that she had done so. The smile changed her, a little.

'Let's get you dressed then,' she said.

The next chamber was much larger than the one in which he had woken. The light was dimmer: a dull glow from the curving walls. There was a circle of inflated seating in the

34

middle of the room. There were two people there. They rose like ghosts as he approached.

At first glance they were exactly like May, with limbs like long sticks and swollen faces that seemed to float above their dark overalls. They came and took his hand, first one, then the other, in a greeting that Paul thought old-fashioned but at least professional. One had dark skin and straight black hair cut to the shoulder. The other had very little hair; what there was of it was grey. Only when they spoke could he be sure that one was a woman and the other a man.

He did not recognize their names at all: 'Vandamme' and 'Lewis'. Names had not featured in his briefings. In that first meeting he saw them as *the dark one* and *the grey one*.

They sat down on the inflated seats. May glided onto the seating beside the grey man, took his hand and curled up against him. She already knew everybody here. She was at ease with all of them. Paul did not know the others and they did not know him. May had said they were 'jumping up and down' to see him, but they were not. They sat upright, formal and stiff, and so did he. He waited for someone to begin.

The man spoke to a point in the wall: 'Record,' he said. There was a faint click.

'Lewis speaking. This is a most significant day in the history of our station. We have been joined by Paul Munro, telemetry executive. It is hard to exaggerate just how eager we have been for his arrival and how much we have been looking forward to him waking up and being with us. For the first time in nine years we are back to full strength.

'Paul has completed his initial checks and appears to be in good health after his journey. He will undergo a short period of convalescence before assuming responsibility for all aspects of radio and laser communication between the station and Earth. At that point he will be able to begin investigating the irregularities in our signals that Earth has reported to us, to confirm the causes and propose solutions. Dr Vandamme and I will be released to concentrate fully on the duties originally assigned to us, but we will be available to support Paul whenever he needs our help. We will depend on him as he will on us. We wish him all success . . .

'Anything anyone wants to add? May? Van?'

'Just that we're so thrilled he's here,' said May.

'Quite. Paul, would you like to say something?'

Paul had stopped listening. The man's speech had gone on far longer than any communication should.

'No,' he said.

'No?' repeated the man, surprised. 'Surely . . .'

'Don't press him, Lewis,' said May. 'He's doing really well.'

'No? Very well then. End Record.'

There was another faint click.

'It's sometimes hard to think what to say when you know it's going to be fired across four and a half billion kilometres of space for Earth to pore over,' said the man wryly. 'But you'll get used to it. Shall we have some coffee? Is it all right for Paul to have coffee, May?'

'Well . . . a little one, maybe.'

'Coffee, Paul?'

Coffee?

What did it mean?

'It's a stimulant,' said the man, who must have read his face. 'We drink it together as we talk. It's a social ritual. It used to be very common on Earth. There are still parts of Earth where they do it, in fact.'

'I'll make it!' said May, bouncing up from where she sat.

'Let me,' said the man.

'Don't be silly. *You* want to talk to Paul.' And she skipped gently away across the chamber. The far wall parted and allowed her through.

Paul sat cradling his spindly limbs in the inflated seat and looked at the two figures opposite him: these two people, with their heads propped on their long and brittle bodies, who would inhabit this place with him. They were sitting on the edge of their seats, watching him as if his presence had some enormous importance for them.

'I expect you have some questions, Paul,' said the man.

Paul leaned forward. 'You . . .' he managed. 'You – commander?'

'I am the station manager. My first and last command here was that we should all be equals. We cooperate with one another, although we have authority in our own spheres. My sphere is the running of the station. May is the doctor. Between us, we cover the whole of ST1. Van does astronomical observation of the main target.'

He looked at the dark woman, who said, 'I also cover ST2.'

'ST2' was Standard Task 2: the search for life forms, evidence of extinct life forms, or failing either, for the conditions that could theoretically support life. It was a task set for all space missions, manned or otherwise, whatever their main target. It was as automatic as Standard Task 1 – to survive and continue to operate. Paul wondered why the grey man had omitted it.

Then he thought what ST2 must mean out here.

Here in the deep, bombarded cold at the edge of the solar system, where life was an accident that had happened four and a half billion kilometres away.

Paul swallowed. He looked around.

'Now I have a question for you, Paul,' said the man.

'Yes,' said Paul.

The man looked levelly at him. Ancient instincts in Paul's brain at once whispered the word *commander*. Commander, even though the man had said he was not.

His head was big and his flesh folded in deep creases on his forehead and beneath his eyes. His dark brows contrasted with the sparse greys of his scalp. His skin was pale but his cheeks and nose were patterned with so many capillaries that they seemed almost pink. His jaw was tight and powerful. There were no veils of figures over his sight, no images, no distractions, none of the thousand other thoughts and messages that would have been flitting all the time across a man's vision on Earth. His eyes were a wintry grey, and made huge by the surrounding rings of flesh that sagged upon his cheeks like the dishes of radio telescopes that peered deep into the voids of space. The signal they emitted could carry a word into the darkest and most protected place of the heart.

Paul thought that he had never, ever, seen anyone look at him as intently as this – eye to eye and straight into the brain.

'You have been sent away from your home to a place where you can only survive if you remain within a space a few tens of metres square,' said the Commander.

'Yes,' said Paul. His throat was dry.

'You have lost eight years of your life while you slept on your way here.'

'Yes.'

'Your body, like ours, has been distorted. Your bones are now brittle. In theory it would be possible for Earth to recover you and for you to be rehabilitated to an extent where you could spend your remaining years at home. In practice, the effort required to get you back would be enormous and the benefit from Earth's point of view would be nil. You will remain here for the rest of your life – however long that may be. We still do not know what effect this gravity has on lifespan.'

'Yes,' said Paul. It was hard to concentrate on these long, slow messages. And it was hard to meet those eyes without looking away. The voice came in pulses, deep and resonant, like waves hitting a shore.

'Before all this happened to you, you had to give up your World Ear.'

Paul's hand went up automatically to the soft hollow behind his right ear. He could feel nothing there. The tiny scar was long gone.

'The unkindest cut of all. You were taken away from all the thousands of people you were connected with. On other stations in the solar system, the World Ear networks are maintained and can link, albeit with some loss of performance, with those on Earth. Here, because of certain local effects, that is not possible. For communication we must rely on speech. And your human acquaintance will from now on be limited to just us, your three colleagues.'

'Yes.'

'My question, Paul, is this. Did you consent?'

Consent? Paul thought.

The first answer that jumped into his head was 'Yes'. Positive feedback. He had expected all the things that the man had listed. He had accepted that they were going to happen to him. He opened his mouth to say it.

Then he stopped. 'Consent' had a specific meaning. When one party on Earth proposed a course of action which a second had the means to prevent, positive feedback from the second party was *necessary* before the action could occur. That was 'consent'. In his case, of course, no feedback had been required. Therefore . . .

Therefore 'No' was the answer.

But 'No' was not the answer. It implied rejection and resistance. That was wrong. That was not what had happened. Confused, he put his hand to his head.

Then he covered his face.

He must answer. May had said he must not just say 'Yes' or 'No'. He saw now why she had said that.

If he had been on Earth it would have been simple! He could have shown it to them: the enormous effort of the project – the demands made on engineers, physicists, biologists, medics, therapists, telemetrists, astronomers; the organization of wealth and time; the dedication of that priceless astronomical window: the ramifications that went on and on in all directions, drawing power and expertise together into one great push focused on getting his body – his and his alone – to the farthest place that man had ever reached. That justified everything he had ever been. That was all the explanation that should have been needed!

Consent? His lifetime was just one out of all the lifetimes' worth that had been expended. He had the required qualifications. He had the resilience. His exceptionally low therapy usage was a matter of record. Even when he had shown the proposal to Her, and had shared her pain and understanding that all their plans were gone for good, he had not had to resort to the standard therapies accessible through his World Ear. She had, but he had not. Not then.

Now he did not have them any more.

'It . . . was best,' he managed.

'You saw that there was a need,' said the man at once. 'We had lost one of our number and you understood why the replacement should be you. But you had to pay a price. Did you consent?'

'It was best,' Paul repeated.

'But did you consent?'

'Is this necessary?' said the woman's voice.

Paul could not see her. He had put his hand in front of his eyes again. He knew that if he removed his hand, he still would not be able to see.

'Paul,' said the man, 'can you tell me?'

His eyes were hot. His cheeks were wet. Something in him wanted to choke. He remembered this.

'Stop!' said the woman suddenly. 'Stop it! He's not ready!'

He remembered this. He remembered a word spoken to him. 'Normal,' he gasped. 'Normal.'

'Oh, we know about tears,' said the man softly.

After a moment he added: 'I'm sorry, Paul. But I'm not surprised. Not at all. I want you to remember that I asked if you had consented. And that you *could not* answer me.'

'I've made the coffee,' said May brightly. 'How do you like it?'

And then: 'Is he all right?'

IV

The aim was to study the gas giant, the vast green-blue globe of hydrogen, helium and hydrocarbons over a core of hot dense fluids and molten rock that swung in the deep cold at the edge of the solar system. Nothing could be constructed on the planet itself, which had no solid surface and huge storm systems with windspeeds of over two thousand kilometres an hour.

But among the clutter of rocks and satellites that circled the giant, at a distance of just over three hundred thousand kilometres from its gassy surface, was a single substantial moon. The moon had almost no atmosphere. Its period of rotation, at approximately six Earth days, coincided with its period of orbit, so that one face was turned permanently towards its parent. Its surface was composed of nitrogen, water and carbon dioxide, all frozen and scored with enormous canyons and narrow ridges. In a process close to that of volcanoes on Earth, liquid nitrogen and ammonia blew from vents in its crust to flow and freeze on the moon's face.

The ice reflected much of what meagre sunlight reached the little planet. The temperature on the surface averaged thirty-eight degrees above absolute zero.

Thirty-eight degrees Kelvin. Minus two hundred and thirty-five degrees Celsius. Water freezes at zero Celsius, mercury at minus thirty-nine, nitrogen at minus two hundred and ten. In the coldest places on Earth molecules still dance with energy. At thirty-eight Kelvin they are almost lifeless, rigid. In certain materials electrical currents flow freely without any resistance at all.

Here, it was deemed, was a suitable platform for a station that would observe the giant planet and its magnetic field. And for reasons that seemed good it was decided that the station should be manned. In that appalling cold, in that miserable crevice of gravity, a seed of life was planted.

A site was chosen on the side of the moon that permanently faced the gas giant. It was in the bottom of a cliff-sided canyon, so that the station should have the best possible protection from impacts by debris careering around the huge planet. Here, long chains of artificial bubbles were laid by robot crawlers, in layer upon layer over the dead surface. The first layers contained nothing. They existed only for insulation. Then further layers were laid, to house equipment, including a small nuclear reactor which was the station's seed-source of energy. Above these was the level habitable by humans – a tiny blob in comparison to the size of the whole station, consisting of only two common chambers, some smaller working and sleeping chambers for the crew, kitchens and the sanitary units, which were of course the smallest of all.

Above this level were further layers of bubbles, thousands of bubbles, housing between them many hundred hectares of algae and lichens to balance the ecosystems which sustained the humans and to provide the basis of their food. They covered the habitable zone and poured out along the canyon floor. Over these were laid two much larger, transparent layers, filled with gases that were kept dense with the extreme cold. By varying the pressure in these layers it was possible to control the rate at which heat from the internal sources of the station was lost through conduction and so to maintain the living quarters at a constant, tolerable temperature. And throughout the station moved working robots, maintenance robots and surface crawlers, passing from bubble to bubble or travelling outwards, through one airlock after another, until at last they emerged beyond the very outer skin of spun fabric onto the desolation of the moon's surface.

Out there were the buried arrays that exploited the differences between the temperature of the surface and deeper layers of ice to suck in energy from a wide area to warm the station. There were enormous mirrors and solar panels, sited along the lip of the canyon to catch the meagre sunlight. Out there too were the instruments that measured the atmosphere and magnetic field of the gas giant, the patient, crawling probes that sounded and bored their way across the moon's surface in their quest for signs of ancient life, and the radio antennae and lasers trained upwards to the small artificial satellite above the moon, which would bounce the station's communications away on their four-hour journey towards the Earth.

The station was a huge thing: a hulking sponge of artificial fabrics, machines and ecosystems, lurking in its crevice like some soft-skinned reef creature. If molten ice welled up from the moon's crust, the station would float upwards until the flows solidified. If a seal malfunctioned, or if by ill-chance some small asteroid fell directly into the canyon and punctured the fabric, the multiple-celled structure would prevent a catastrophic loss of warmth and pressure. It was a creation of great ingenuity, achieved in the face of staggering physical challenges of transport and construction, to protect and nurse the four tiny lives within it.

And yet it had already failed once.

Lewis spoke a command. The ceiling of the bubble went dark.

'Ugh,' said May.

The gas giant hung in the space above them: a misty blue half-disc, swimming in a great starless blackness that stretched the length of the ceiling. The blackness was marbled by grey wisps that must have been thin clouds of crystals floating in the near-vacuum of the moon's atmosphere. Above and below the giant, uneven silvery lines marked the glitter of ice on either lip of the canyon. And outside these the screen showed the solid blackness of the cliff wall.

'It's like an eye, isn't it?' said May. 'Makes me shiver.'

Perhaps it was. The pale half-disc was the right shape, widening perceptibly as the moon swung round towards its sunlit side. But the white of the eye was not white: it was blue. And there was no iris, no pupil.

'Blind,' Paul said.

'Wait till you see it with a storm system on it,' said May. 'A great dark blob the size of this moon or bigger, yeah? It's just like an eye then. And sometimes it's looking straight at us.'

Paul put up an arm, sighting along it to his clenched fist and to the shape that hung in the sky. His fist was not big enough to cover the disc. He put up both fists, pressing them together at the knuckles and the heel of the palm. That covered it – just.

'The planet is fifty thousand kilometres in diameter,' said Lewis, watching him. 'From here, that gives you ten degrees of arc.'

On Earth Paul could have covered the full moon with the tip of his little finger. And yet the giant still looked small in that blackness.

'There's an ocean up there that you could sink the Earth in,' said Lewis. 'And poach it too. At the lower levels the temperature reaches thousands of degrees.'

Paul looked away. His eyes found a silvery mark on the near cliff-face. It seemed to be some sort of ledge that dropped diagonally downwards from the top. It was too straight to be natural. On Earth it would have been a path.

'That line?' he asked.

'That's the Highway – the track our crawlers use when we want to get them up on that side. Seventy per cent of it follows a fault in the ice. The constructors only had to improve it in places. There's nothing like it on the other side. If we want to send anything in that direction it has to go six kilometres down the canyon to Chesapeake and then back along the top.'

The crew had littered the landscape with names. 'Chesapeake' was where the canyon opened, in a great bay of ice that had somehow reminded someone of the beautiful blue waters of home. There were others: 'Boston' and

'Humperdinck' and 'Cattle Grid' and 'Rain Tree', each of which described some deathly barren feature on the surface that was nothing but ice and unimaginable cold.

'And that?' asked Paul.

There was a bright, angular shape at the canyon edge, near to where the 'Highway' reached it. It stuck up like a needle, catching the light of the planet. It might have been an antenna but it was not.

'That's Thorsten,' said May after a moment's pause.

'The cairn is covered with ice now,' Lewis added. 'But we put that pylon there so we'll know where he is.'

'Yes,' said Paul. He noticed that Lewis had said *he* where he should have said *it*. But it was a small discrepancy and his meaning seemed clear.

Then he saw the way that Lewis was looking at him. They were all looking at him.

'Thorsten Bondevik,' said Lewis. 'Your predecessor. That's where he's buried.'

'. . . Yes,' said Paul.

Then he said, 'What was the accident?'

'Accident?' repeated the one called Vandamme.

'Thorsten.'

'Thorsten's death was not an accident,' said Lewis slowly. 'Weren't you told?'

Paul frowned. 'They said . . . accident.'

There was a short silence.

'It just doesn't happen on Earth any more,' said Vandamme.

'It does, still,' said Lewis. 'But in the more developed networks, almost never.'

'But to call it an accident!' May protested. 'That makes it *our* fault!'

'No?' said Paul.

'It was not an accident, Paul,' said Lewis. 'He killed himself.'

Paul frowned. Then he blinked, deliberately. Nothing came. (Of course it did not – he had forgotten.) He felt a dizziness in his brain – a shift of balance, as if his mind had somehow drifted further from his feet than it should have done. He tried to think.

He thought that yes, a man could damage his own body. If that damage was severe he would die. That would still be an accident, of course.

Unless . . .

Lewis said, 'Restore ceiling.'

The blackness above them vanished. The great planet was gone. The view of that vast emptiness was replaced by the opaque creamy light of the living quarters – a plain, arched chamber with eight doors off it. But the words Paul had heard still wandered in his mind, trying and trying and finding no answer. He looked around helplessly.

'Why?' he asked.

'He became depressed, Paul,' said Lewis. 'I don't suggest we go over the history now. I'll brief you on it another time.'

Paul nodded. He turned to May.

'Why did he kill himself?'

May and Lewis exchanged glances.

'He just got lonely, Paul,' May said. 'And frustrated. He used to spend hours looking at the walls. We didn't realize what was wrong because to start with he had adapted better than any of us . . .'

The woman called Vandamme was still watching him. There was something about the way she was standing there while the other two answered his questions.

Paul asked her, 'Why did Thorsten kill himself?'

'Paul . . .' said Lewis.

Vandamme's hand moved to her collar. It played with the fabric there.

'May's talking to you,' she said. 'Why do you ask me?'

'He didn't mean it like that, Van,' said May hurriedly.

'He didn't think of it as interrupting,' said Lewis. 'Paul, what May says is correct. Thorsten became depressed. He preferred to die rather than go on living here. We had thought this would be included in your briefing but evidently it was—'

Paul said to her again, 'Why did Thorsten kill himself?'

'Oh God!' muttered Vandamme.

'Just give him a *chance*, yeah?' said May. 'He's putting it for confirmation, to all of us, the same as he would on Earth. He doesn't realize—'

'What is God?' said Paul.

Lewis snorted. It might have been a laugh. 'One thing at a time, Paul, shall we?'

'It's the World Ear,' said May. 'Don't you remember what it was like?'

'We weren't like this,' said Vandamme quietly.

She had turned her head sideways a little so that now she was watching him from the corners of her eyes. Her mouth was a short straight line. She was frowning a little.

She was a tall woman, a head taller than May. She might have been the same height as Paul, although it was hard to tell because both of them were bouncing lightly on their tiptoes in the low gravity. Her eyes were large and dark. He sensed a great depth to them, as if the light that entered her pupils still had to travel a long, long way before it reached the person within.

She said, 'It was good to meet you, Munro. I am glad you have come. Though I suppose you may not be.'

Of all of these strange people, he thought, she was the strangest. She was the strangest because she spoke the least.

And unlike May and Lewis, she called him 'Munro' – the second and more formal part of his name. 'Vandamme' must be the equivalent for her. If she had an informal name, she did not expect others to use it – not even her colleagues, who would be out here with her for the rest of their lives.

'I have things to do now,' she said.

She skipped slowly away from him, covering three or four metres in each glide, and came to rest by a seal at the far end of the room.

'Van . . .' May called after her.

Vandamme touched the control with her hand. The seal opened with a hiss. Paul glimpsed a small, brightly lit airlock beyond. Then the seal closed behind her, restoring the unbroken glow of the wall.

'Where has she gone?' asked Paul.

'Only to her chamber,' said Lewis.

'That's one thing about being here,' said May. 'We can't go very far, however bad we feel.'

Paul frowned. 'I have . . . offended her?'

'Thorsten was her partner,' said Lewis bluntly. 'But I suppose that wasn't in your briefings either.'

Her partner!

Of course he would have been.

There were so many cues that he was missing! There should have been alerts about the man Thorsten – and about

Vandamme – before he came to this meeting. With the World Ear he could have guessed at Vandamme's mood from the way she framed her messages and from the colours she used in them. And there were other cues too that were present but that he was maybe not interpreting correctly: the way Lewis and May stood looking at the seal through which Vandamme had gone; the way Lewis spoke, as if his mind was only partly on what he was saying; the frown on May's face . . . They had been hoping for something. It hadn't happened. What had it been?

'Sorry,' he said.

'Don't worry about it,' said May. She sounded suddenly bitter. 'That's just Van being Van. It happens.'

'We can't expect too much,' said Lewis sombrely. 'At this stage. But, Paul – please remember, you cannot use speech as you would the World Ear. You cannot have simultaneous conversations. Everyone will hear everything you say. And if I am speaking to you, I do not expect you to interrupt me. Concentrate on what I am saying. It will seem long to you but please concentrate! *Then* you may reply.'

'It helps to look at whoever's speaking too,' said May.

'Slow,' grumbled Paul.

'Yes, it *is* slow,' snapped Lewis. 'It's also more skilful, more entertaining, superior in many ways! And it's what we do, Paul. I'm sorry but you'll have to get used to it!'

'And be careful about God,' said May. 'It's important to Van, yeah?'

Lewis snorted again.

'You all right, Paul?' said May. 'You want to rest?'

Paul shook his head angrily. 'I want to work,' he said.

V

Within a few hours of his waking he knew the place where he was to spend the rest of his life. Four work-chambers opened off the main common room, two on each side. There was also a little kitchen, and opposite it the sanitary unit. At one end of the long chamber was an airlock leading to the outer layers of the station. At the other was another airlock, this time leading to another suite of living quarters where the woman Vandamme worked and slept alone.

And that was all.

The work-chambers were identical in size and shape: globes some four metres in diameter with a floor inserted about a third of the way up to give purchase for the feet. Hand-holds studded the walls at intervals. Each pair of work-chambers had a little two-person sleeping cell sited between them. One of these work-and-sleeping suites was his. It was different from the one that May and Lewis inhabited only in that he had not yet set any displays, so the walls and ceiling of his three rooms were all blank.

It was slightly cooler too. The light had a shimmery, misty quality. Tiny beads of moisture were gathering on one area of the wall. It was Paul's own breath, condensing on the cold surface as he sat in his little capsule of dense, warm air. The shimmering of the light told him what the wall concealed: that behind that glowing barrier the temperature fell sharply (and at this moment was probably even lower than it should be). Beyond the wall lay another chamber, one where the air was too thin and cold for a human to survive unaided. And beyond that would be another, and another, each with a pressure and a temperature that was lower than the last, until finally there was nothing but the skin of the station and the enormous, frozen void outside.

'Munro?' said a voice at his door.

'Yes!' He answered more loudly than necessary because he was surprised. There was a slight draught of air as she came in.

Paul had been expecting a visitor. He had agreed with Lewis that he would be shown the station communications at precisely this time. He had not been expecting Vandamme.

'Where is Lewis?' he asked.

'He says he has tests to run. He has asked me to do your induction.'

She crossed to the far wall and ran her finger down it.

'This is bad,' she said, peering at the wetness on her finger tip. 'You should report it.'

Paul looked away from her. He still did not like to look at the human form in this place, to see how brittle and thin her limbs were, and how large and puffy her face. He was unsettled too. Yesterday they had spoken and she had walked away. The connection between them had been affected by his blunder about the man Thorsten. Now he would have to repair it. He was not used to this. If he had met with such a difficulty on Earth, he would simply have dropped that connection and opened others to compensate. There always had been others, there.

'I am sorry I offended you,' he said.

'You did not offend me,' she replied.

Neither his words nor her answer seemed to be enough. He was not sure how to proceed.

'Please sit down,' he said.

'Sure. I was going to.' She settled beside him, folding up her thin limbs as if she were folding a tripod. They were both tense.

'So – you want to get started?'

'Yes,' he said.

'I thought you were going to be on rehab for a week.'

'I am. But I want to work. Work is . . . good.'

She thought about it for a moment. Then she nodded. 'Yes,' she said. 'It is.'

A command, spoken to a wall receiver, brought a control console rising out of a hatch in the floor. The equipment was supported on a flexible arm that could be drawn to any point in the room. It consisted of a microphone, a joystick and an array of mechanical keys patterned with letters, numbers and symbols.

'Screen,' said Vandamme. Opposite them, a long oval of wall changed colour. 'That's the working area. You can adjust it if you want. Now, you see that alert?'

In the bottom right-hand corner of the screen area, a small red rectangle was blinking on and off. On it was an acronym that Paul did not recognize.

'You get one of those, you need to report it. That'll be because the system is picking up the condensation here.'

'So . . . we tell Lewis?'

'In a moment. We'll look at the comms first. Lists.'

A column, composed mostly of words, appeared on the screen.

'Comms,' said Vandamme.

The column was replaced by a much shorter one.

Int
Ex-L
Ex-R

'Interior comms is inside the station. You can call up any of the living chambers, the airlocks and any of the headsets that we might be wearing if we suit up to go into the outer areas of the station. So you can speak to anyone at any time – though if we're off watch, we might be asleep.'

'Yes,' said Paul. He had remembered that he should be looking at her as they spoke. He should be acknowledging her messages with his eyes as well as his voice. He was trying to do this.

But she was not returning his looks. This confused him. He did not know if he was acting incorrectly, or if she was. Her voice continued in a level stream of words.

'Ex-L is the laser. That carries most of our communications to Earth. Ex-R is the radio. That's for communications to crawlers and other equipment out on the surface. It also relays our radio observation data to Earth, and any other remotely gathered data that's transmitted in to us by radio. It's a backup in case there's ever a pointing error on the laser. Both the laser and the radio go via the comms satellite, because our horizon down in the bottom of this pit is pretty well non-existent.'

Paul gave up and looked at the instruments instead. What he saw disgusted him. A screen, a joystick – even a keyboard! The World Ear had been making equipment like this obsolete when he was born. He hoped fervently that he would never have to use the keyboard. He knew he could not spell.

'How do you send?' he said.

'You can type, speak or select. Speaking is easiest, especially for internals.' She clicked the joystick twice. Symbols flickered briefly on the screen. 'Hello?'

'Hello?' said Lewis's voice.

'We're in Munro's work-chamber. There's an alert. Condensation on the north wall.'

'Shit! Why's that happening?' There was a pause. Lewis, in one of the other chambers in the living quarters, must have been checking some readings. 'That shouldn't be happening,' he said. 'I'll look into it.'

'Thank you,' said Vandamme. She clicked the joystick again. 'And that's how you sign off,' she said.

Paul was looking at the screen. Words had appeared there. He puzzled through them and found that they were a record of the short conversation between Lewis and Vandamme.

'He thinks it is our shit?'

'No. That's just an exclamation. It is to give force to what is said. In the World Ear you would have used colour or music, I think. He likes to say things the way they used to

62

be said. He says "shit" and "damn" when he's angry. He also says "God" but he doesn't mean it. He even quotes scripture at me,' she finished sourly. 'Like to try the externals now?'

'Yes.'

'We'll report to Earth that you've declared yourself operational.' She clicked the joystick again. 'This goes out over the laser. Again you have a choice of type or voice. For a message to Earth, I usually type. It makes me think about what I'm saying.' Her fingers flickered on the keys. *TR1: 21:03:0437 Telmex operational.*

'TR1?'

'Our call sign. "Telmex" is you – the telemetry executive. The numbers are the date-time group, which is Zulu-time on Earth. It means nothing here, but the systems insist on it.'

'Yes.'

'Would you like to send?' She offered him the joystick.

He reached for it. *Click.* A group of laser pulses began a long journey through space.

'They answer in – eight hours?'

'Maybe a bit more. The satellite will fire it as soon as Earth's over its horizon. And there'll be an acknowledgement, yes. But if we ask for anything complicated it may take days for Earth to reply.'

'Why so long?' Paul asked sharply.

'Does that bother you? I suppose it would. All that

messaging – it may be very quick when you're in it. But seen from out here it can take days for Earth to build up a response. Sorry, Munro. That's the way it is.'

She still had not looked at him – not once, since stepping into his chamber.

Paul shifted. He frowned at the screen. He thought of the chamber beyond the wall, and the ones beyond that, and then . . .

Four hours at light speed. He could never go back.

He gripped his knees.

'When we drink coffee?' he asked.

'When you like. I will not.'

'With others.'

'Oh – hours yet. You'll be off watch when the others come back on. But you can join them if you want to.'

Hours!

'We send another,' he said firmly.

'Another message?'

'Yes!'

'Who to?'

Who? To anyone! To everyone he could! And receive back! Build a network – that was what he wanted to do. To give and receive as much as possible!

'To . . . my partner,' he said.

Her eyes widened. And now, for the first time, she turned to face him.

'Your partner?' she repeated.

'She can receive, I think.'

'Yes. But—' She stopped. She dropped her eyes, frowning.

'I must not?' he asked.

She shook her head. She bit her lip. 'Sure you can,' she said. 'If you want. But . . . it's been eight years for her, hasn't it? Will it feel the same to her as it does to you?'

'No. I know that.'

She looked at him again. He saw the swollen face, the narrow neck – every wound left by this gravity was there for his examination. Those marks were on him too.

'Won't she have someone else by now? Through the matching systems?'

'Yes of course.' On Earth there was no need to be alone if you did not want to be alone.

But that was on Earth.

'All right,' she said at last. 'If you think it's right. Classify it "Personal" and they'll know what to do with it at the other end.'

Paul faced the screen. He took the joystick and picked the laser. The screen, a pale, blue oval, waited for him. He looked at the keyboard. Then he remembered that he could speak his commands. 'Message,' he said.

Instantly the screen responded: *TR1: 21:03:0441 . . .*

'Personal,' he said. 'Romeo Echo Alfa Two Six Two Five Point Two One Eight' – crazy, that he must spell out her reference like that! – 'I have arrived. I am well . . .'

He hesitated.

'I want you . . .'

'No you don't,' said Vandamme. 'You don't want her to be here. Not if you still love her.'

He thought about it.

'No,' he said, 'you are right.'

And because the machine was receiving voice, the screen now read:

TR1: 21:03:0441 Personal. REA2625.218 I have arrived. I am well. I want you. No you don't. You don't want her to be here. Not if you still love her. No you are right.

Stupid! Clumsy!

'You mean "I miss you",' sighed Vandamme.

You mean I miss you appeared on the screen. Paul swallowed. He felt as if the little cold droplets from his wall had started to form inside his throat. Deliberately he controlled the joystick to remove the unnecessary words. He left *I miss you.* Then he sent the message. *Click.* It disappeared.

The screen showed him nothing.

And nothing.

And nothing.

Of course there would be no answer. Not yet. There couldn't be.

(Four hours – just to get there!)

Vandamme was waiting for him.

She was waiting for him with her arms folded and her eyes fixed on the chamber wall. A moment ago he thought he had sensed a response from her, just the faintest sympathy, as he fired all his love and his loss over the vastness of space. But it was gone now. Now she was like an adult waiting for a child to finish some game – patient, but remote from what he was doing. To her it had been pointless.

There were nine billion people in orbit around the Sun. None of them were responding to him. He could pour his words out over the lasers – *I am lonely, I need help* – in endless repetition. He could run out into the vacuum and die screaming it at the planet overhead. There would be no answer. And there was no answer, either, from the woman beside him. The screen still showed nothing.

'Tell me about the problem,' he said.

'The problem?'

'The radio.'

'Oh, that. You want to get started right away?'

'Yes!'

She shrugged. 'All right,' she said. 'So, it's the radio systems. I guess you must have been briefed on the basics before you came. We have an intermittent loss of data on the radio transmissions to Earth.'

Yes, they had told him. They had filled him with it – the patterns of loss, the small percentage of groups known to be corrupted, the far larger percentages of groups that were suspect because it was known that corruptions could occur. They had told him all of it. It was the whole reason why he had been sent. And now he was here, eight years later, with all that effort behind him. And the crew replied, '*Oh, that.*'

'What . . .?' he began painfully.

'What causes it? We don't know for sure. Most of the time everything's fine. But about once an orbit, something goes wrong and we lose a few groups. It's probably charging on the satellite, caused by the planet's magnetic field.'

Paul frowned. 'Show me,' he said.

Vandamme turned to the controls. 'Graph,' she said. 'Planetary readings. Current.'

Jiggling lines appeared on the screen. Paul looked at them.

'Low?' he said.

'At this point in the orbit, yes. But it fluctuates—'

'No,' said Paul.

68

Of course the satellite could be picking up a charge as it followed the moon round and round on its journey through the magnetic field. And at some point that charge would be released, sending phantom signals through the satellite's systems and maybe even damaging components. But the levels Paul was looking at were too low to worry him.

Vandamme shrugged. 'Not at the moment, no. But when we get round to the tail there's a region that's highly active. You know what a substorm is?'

'Substorm?'

'We get them in Earth's field from time to time. The solar wind distorts the planet's magnetic field. It compresses it on the sunward side and pushes it out into a long tail on the dark side, like the tail of a comet, yes?' She drew an imaginary shape in the air. 'All right. So sometimes, in Earth's field, this magnetic tail gets snapped in two – pinched out by the solar wind. Then the lines of force on the Earth side flow back violently towards the Earth. That's what we call a substorm – like an eddy in a stream. In Earth's field they happen in ones or twos and they're not long-lived. Here, there's a region with *thousands* of these eddies. We skim one edge of it every time we orbit the dark side of the planet. And the currents around these eddies whip up high levels of energy, like the winds around a hurricane . . .'

Paul listened with growing horror.

'. . . I can't figure it out. Somehow it's achieved a kind of stability. The outer eddies are not dispersing at once, so they have time to act on the inner systems, which then divide, replacing the outer ones when they are lost. But there must be something that keeps it going. It could be the solar wind – though that's weak out here. Or it could be some property of the planetary core, which isn't like Earth's core at all. Anyway, these patterns just copy and copy themselves, boiling away in the wake of the planet. They're unique. And they're strong. Early observations missed the region altogether, so the satellite wasn't designed for the charge that would build up—'

'No!'

He had almost screamed it at her. She froze.

'What is the matter?'

'It is not the field,' he said. 'It is not.'

'Why not?'

'Because . . .' He concentrated.

He thought through all that he remembered of the briefings he had received on Earth. He had not tried to memorize them, because they would have been passed to the station's Knowledge Store. But the main direction had been clear to him – as clear as the huge thrust of effort that was to carry him out here. The station systems, their susceptibilities, the possibilities of subtle interference from one to another, the habits of the crew – he knew where Earth expected him to look.

'If it is the field,' he said, 'I can do nothing.'

He could not reach into the orbits above the moon. He could not bolt more insulation onto the little relay station that swung through the sky. If it was the action of the field upon the satellite, Earth should have sent out a new and better-designed satellite.

If it was the field, they should not have sent a man at all.

'Thorsten spent months looking,' Vandamme said quietly. 'In the end he eliminated everything – except the field.'

'Earth does not think it is the field,' Paul said.

'Earth can't tell. Its data isn't complete—'

'*Aarh!*' Paul screamed. He hit his knee with his fist.

'Munro!'

He closed his eyes. He opened them. When he shifted in his seat, his body rose slightly in the low gravity. The screen was before him, blank.

'I will find it,' he said.

And he added, 'Thank you.'

She was waiting for him again. But there was no more to say.

'You're done with me, are you?' she said. 'You don't need me any more?'

'Yes, thank you.'

'Well,' she said. 'If you're done with me, I'll go.'

Maybe she was offended again. Maybe she did not care. He could not tell from her voice.

And he did not care either. Not now. Not any more. He was consumed by the need to hunt the thing he had been sent here to find, so that he could prove to himself that there was a reason for him to be here after all. An emptiness was opening inside him. He felt it – a deep, cold gulf, with a voice inside it that was beginning to howl like an animal.

'Munro,' she said softly from the door.

'Yes?'

'It is all right to cry.'

He looked up at her.

'It is all right to cry,' she repeated, as if she were suggesting a series of tests he might run on the systems.

His jaw clenched. 'We cry too much.'

'You think so? "By the waters of Babylon we sat down and wept." That was exile. So is this. Why shouldn't we cry? We can cry because we're as God means us to be.'

She stopped and looked at the floor. He knew what she was doing. It was something he did himself, all the time now. She was hunting for words.

'Why don't people on Earth cry?' she said. 'It's not just those therapy routines that kick in the moment their pulse

72

rate starts rising. It's because all their lives their brains have been conditioned to being part of something – something far bigger than they are – and so the things that happen to *them* don't seem to matter so much. That's not what we're meant to be.'

'Meant?'

She sighed. 'You don't believe in God, do you?'

He had looked this up in the station Knowledge Store after their first meeting. The Knowledge Store had said that belief in a god had once been required for the propagation of accepted social and political behaviour. It was now obsolete.

He had also started to read the entries that she had recorded alongside this. She had written entry after entry. They were not facts or observations or conclusions. They were stories – things that other people had written and that she was writing again from memory. They were things that could not be true, but she believed them. She believed them because she believed in God.

That was what she did, watch in, watch out, when she was not sleeping or working. She went to her chamber and wrote things that could not be true.

'No,' he said.

'Then I'm sorry,' she said. 'Because you have no one but yourself here. That is difficult. That is very difficult.'

VI

The Sun was tiny. Seen from a distance of four and a half billion kilometres, the power that drove all life, all energy, all the orbits around it, was no more than a brilliant point like a star. And the star was setting.

Paul had called up the external view on his chamber display so that he could watch the eclipse. The crescent of the great planet above him had slimmed to the finest curved line, with the star touching on it like a tiny, brilliant diamond on a huge ring. The rest of the planet was solid black, the field it swam in was a misty black, and only the faintest traceries of reflected light showed where the blackness of planet and sky gave way to the sheltering cliffs around the station. The marker of Thorsten's grave shone dully, like a needle in firelight.

The star sank towards the planet. As it sank it carried with it, tucked away in the vast nothingness around it, all the world he had known. There went the humming life, the constant flickering busyness that he had felt every waking hour. There went the rainforests, the blue oceans and skies – the things he had hardly ever looked at when he was among them. And She went with them too, in her little bubble-house by the shore, sad but still living in the communities of the World Ear.

She had not replied to his message. He had sent another, with images of the station, and asking for images of herself and the boy. He had found that he desperately wanted to see what the child looked like. He needed to see that there was a copy of himself, planted in the rich warm soil of Earth where it could grow. It would have helped him. She must have had that message too by now. There had been no answer.

The last light was fading. The diamond was merging into the ring. The ring itself seemed to grow brighter for a few moments, and then to diminish. The spark was drowning in blackness. It was nearly gone.

Still it seemed to hesitate, on the brink of its death. The faint brightness clung to the rim of the black disc longer than Paul thought possible. And for a few moments he imagined that it was still there, even after it had gone. His eyes hunted for ghosts of the spark in the field that was entirely black. Black, black, and all those distances of kilometres and hundreds of thousands of kilometres and billions of kilometres were all melded into one flat blackness that had no depth and no meaning. He had been looking at a point of light, no more.

Roughly he swung himself back to his work. On his wall-screen he had laid out the latest steps in his hunt for the fault – the time groups of the messages known to have been corrupted, the extent of the corruption, the firing patterns of the main and auxiliary radio transmitters, and the transmitter specifications. Some ten per cent of radio-to-Earth transmissions in his sample had been affected. Sometimes just a few groups had been lost, sometimes it was as much as fifty per cent of the transmission. He could find no radio messages from Earth that had been corrupted. But then Earth only used the radio for the automatic acknowledgements of radio messages from the station.

The corruptions peaked at approximately six-day intervals. The last had been about five days ago, shortly before his waking.

He prepared a test message to Earth.

TR1: 24:03:0802 Test. From Telmex. Repeat following groups by radio. UINK 2298 RPER 5159 TXRE 0198 . . .

He sent it, noted the time group and called up the log of energy use in the station – the transmitters, pressurizers, heating units, computers, sanitary units and kitchens. He logged the state of the reactor. He did not try to guess whether any of the activity levels were unusual. He would repeat the exercise every eight hours. When Earth reported a corruption he would go back through his records and see if there was a spike from any of the station energy sources that might have caused the interference.

For completeness he logged the exterior temperature of the station. Thirty-six Kelvin. He did not think about what that meant.

He logged the atmospheric pressure (negligible).

Then he called up the magnetic field readings, meaning to project them in a line graph. The graph axes displayed themselves promptly. But there were no readings.

No readings?

He muttered to himself and clicked the manual control. *Back*. And *Graph* and *Planetary Readings, Current* again.

Nothing was showing – nothing at all.

It was on, all right. But it was displaying nothing.

Then something flicked in the top right-hand corner of the screen area. A yellow line, down and up.

A fault?

Or a reading of something much higher than the default was set to record?

Right up there? A *low* point on the reading?

He called up the numbers that underlay the graphics. When he saw them he grunted aloud.

They were high. They were far higher than he had expected – or wanted – to see. He stared at them helplessly. The numbers reeled away in impossible quantities.

Impossible?

Consult!

Lewis was on watch. He called up Lewis's chamber.

'Lewis!'

'Paul?' said Lewis's voice. 'Yes, what is it?'

'The field readings!'

'What about them?'

'They are . . . too big.'

'Let's see what you're looking at.' There was a short silence as Lewis adjusted his workstation to let him see what was on Paul's.

'I have changed the scale,' said Paul. 'But . . .'

'You should change it again,' said Lewis. 'I find one point eight to minus one point two captures most of it.'

'This is normal?'

'We're traversing the tail of the planetary field. We observe these fluctuations every time. So yes, it's normal. But it's also unique. You don't get this structure anywhere else in the solar system – not stable, like this. Impressive, isn't it?'

The reading dropped sharply. It plunged past the horizontal axis and carried on down.

'That flow has . . . changed!'

'Reversed. Yes, it does. Keep watching and it will reverse again.'

'It is harmful?'

'Harmful?' Lewis seemed to think for a moment. 'Eventually, yes. The field traps particles from the solar wind. It whips them up to high levels of energy, as you see. Prolonged exposure to that would certainly be harmful. It came as a shock to Earth when it finally understood just what levels we could experience in this region. Early observations of the tail had made it seem pretty quiet.'

'If it was harmful, they would have aborted?'

'Earth wasn't going to abort – not after it had got as far as it had. It put an extra gas layer onto the station to give us that bit more stopping distance. The in-place systems got some extra shielding and the station as a whole got some extra redundancy. The one thing it couldn't shield was the World Ear. There's no way a World Ear can interact with the nervous system through half a centimetre of metal, is there? So this station, alone of all the stations in the solar system, runs without it. And we run fine – except that every now and then it gets too much for the radio systems and our comms to Earth get interrupted—'

'That is not the field,' said Paul.

'I don't know what else it could be, Paul.'

'Earth does not think it is the field!'

There was a pause.

'You'd better come over,' said Lewis. 'We need to talk.'

'If it was the field, I would not have been sent.'

'Paul . . . this is difficult. When you and I see something happen to someone, we look for a cause, and we expect that cause to make sense to us. Why not? *We* are still humans, after all. What we have to understand is that Earth looks at things very differently. Just because our loss happened to be the telemetry executive doesn't mean—'

'Stop!' said Paul roughly.

Silence. He swallowed. 'You say we are still human. You mean everyone else is not?'

Again Lewis paused.

'That's exactly what I mean, Paul,' he said slowly. 'We – the four of us here – are, or soon will be, the only humans left.'

Paul said nothing.

'We are the only humans left,' Lewis repeated. 'The billions on Earth are no longer *humans*. They are no longer rational beings who think for themselves. They have become joined into something much larger. They have become part of a single, gigantic consciousness. That is the World Ear.'

Silence, so thick that Paul could hear the faint hum of his wall-display. He heard Lewis draw breath over the intercom. He drew breath himself and held it.

'I don't agree,' he said.

'Then you'd better come over,' snapped Lewis. '*You* may not need eye contact for this, but I do!'

Lewis needed eye contact, Paul thought, because without it his words would only be words – easily considered and dismissed. But his eyes added to what he said. Paul felt them waiting for him even as he crossed the common room. Powerful and grey, circled in their rings of flesh, they met him as he entered Lewis's work-chamber. They pointed him towards the inflated seat. ('Sit down,' said Lewis.) And when he had sunk into it, feeling hollow and a little tense, they rested upon him like hands placed lightly on his shoulders, as if they could lock with great strength and pin him down when he tried to rise. Paul looked away. He looked around the room.

He saw that the chamber was the same size and shape as every other work-chamber in the station. But every square metre of wall was set to display a different image. There were tall white buildings, shining in the sun against a blue sky. There were ships under sail on a wide sea. There was a man directing other men, who walked in rows and wore the same old-fashioned clothes. There was a courtyard of an old brick-built house, with yellow-painted woodwork and the sunlight filtering down through dusty air and a woman sitting doing something that involved straw. From time to time one would change to another, unhurriedly, but with a lazy power that implied a million other images waiting to be shown, all things that had been done by people, great things and little things that the watching eye must never forget.

Paul wondered why so many of the images were from long ago.

'So,' said Lewis. 'Tell me what you think.'

'On Earth,' said Paul, 'I knew who I was. I thought. I was not a . . . a . . .'

'Slave?'

'Slave, yes. I was not a slave. That is one point.'

'That was your perception. But—'

Paul hurried on. 'I know. You say I could not "consent". Of course I did "consent". I came. I did not fight.'

'Neither did any of us,' said Lewis dryly.

'Lewis – the World Ear is a tool! A' – he fumbled for the words – 'a communications tool. It is not even a computer. It is—'

He broke off, still hunting for words that would not come. Lewis supplied them.

'It is simply a fusion of earlier technologies: the internet,

82

mobile telephone, computing, look-up displays and speakers that resonate against the earbones – a useful device and no more. Is that what you want to say?'

'Yes. A machine. We built it. We switch it on. We control it. It is not a brain. You cannot build and switch on brains. They are because of—' He stopped again, frustrated. 'I am bad at this!' he hissed.

'For someone who could barely speak only a few days ago, you're doing very well. And the word you want is "Evolution". Generations of adaptation and feedback from the environment – that's what makes a brain. Yes?'

'Yes. And not everyone has a World Ear. Only half, when I left Earth.'

Lewis bowed his head. The wrinkles ran like little waves at his neck. His cheeks were hollow.

'When I left Earth, Paul, it was just under thirty per cent. So it had doubled, nearly, in ten years. It has been another eight years since then. Judging by the downloads that came in while you were on your way, I should say that coverage is around eighty per cent and increasing. Of course there are still rejectionists and isolated communities. There are people who would die rather than accept the World Ear. But they *will* die, and their children or their grandchildren will accept it. A rejectionist community on Earth has no more hope of long-term survival now than did the Stone Age jungle tribes we were still trying to preserve at the start of this century. Before long every capable adult will be participating in these networks. And the We is being fitted to children at around their first birthday. Generations are growing up with no need to speak, Paul. What will that do to their evolving brains?'

'The *We*?'

'The We. W-E. World Ear. That's what we call it here. Although when we say "the We" we really mean the thing that is created when billions of brains are all linked by the World Ear.' He pulled a face. 'You can imagine why it's happening. With simple self-training programs designed for children, the World Ear can allow an infant to begin communicating at a basic level within a few months. How long does it take a child to learn to talk? Do you know – I've no idea! I'm looking forward—'

He checked himself and shook his head. For a moment he simply floated, bouncing lightly upon his toes, staring into the air. His face was set. Then he began to skip gently around the room.

'You are looking forward . . .?' Paul prompted. He was intrigued by Lewis's momentary loss of concentration.

Lewis ignored him. 'May says that when you first spoke with her, you could only answer "Yes" or "No". Do you remember?'

Paul shifted in his seat. 'I was not used to talking. As you said.'

'Of course not. You had to simplify your messages to the very essence of what you wanted to convey. But that only makes it clearer. After half a lifetime within the World Ear your habit of thought was almost binary. You received the input, assessed it and signalled yes or no. You will be doing the same now, as I speak.'

'Yes. And I am signalling "No".'

Lewis's mouth twitched. 'And that's how the brain cell behaves. Through the World Ear you had – what – a thousand regular connections? More than that?'

'What is "regular"?'

'That you contacted every few days.'

'Yes. Maybe as many as a thousand.'

'Which is approximately the same number of connections performed by a single brain cell – not a human brain cell, to be sure, but one of a highly developed animal.'

Paul stared at him.

'Don't make the mistake of thinking a brain has to be a mass of nerve tissue, Paul. It's a complex, restless structure of pathways, connections, feedback, some reinforced by constant use, others that are almost valueless . . . It's not a computer, no. Of course not. Its operations are quite different. But, Paul – did you ever make a decision by yourself back on Earth? Without consulting? I doubt it. All your knowledge, most of your experience, was provided to you through the We. You had no meaning without it. What were you, if not part of it? What use was all your training? Who would ever consult you? Consent? How could you?'

His eyes held Paul's, trapped in those concentric rings of flesh.

'I'll tell you what happened, Paul. I remember my case and I saw some of yours. Sure, the astronomical observers on Earth were getting gaps in our data. They did not like that. It made their job harder. It also hurt the theoretical labs who use our readings. They reported it. They did not say, "Send Paul Munro." They said, "Gap in data." They kept reporting it. It came up at the teleconferences. Archives were consulted. They said, "Station has no telemetrist" – Thorsten had killed himself. Other archives said, "When we lost specialists on other stations, we sent replacements" . . .'

His hand moved through the air. Behind him, the pictures shifted on to the next with the same easy rhythm.

'I'm simplifying, of course. But do you see how like a brain it functions? By this time planning departments were considering the distance to our station – again consulting archives about the expedition that got us here. They could calculate what would be needed. Still the messages came out of the conferences saying, "Station is undermanned. This is important." This is the key, Paul. Lots of things get put to conferences, but this one came up often enough and affected enough things for the networks to say, "This is important." More networks paid attention. Other distractions were filtered out. Resources were matched to the task. And archives were consulted again – for a person, this time. One with specific qualifications, who could also pass specific personality tests. You.

'At no point, Paul – *at no point* – did anyone say, "Is it worth sending Paul Munro off to a barren, frozen rock for the rest of his life?" There was no one with that function! Archives gave the information they were asked for. It was not their place to judge. Planners said what would be necessary. It was not their place to judge. And when the message came to you, *you did not ask it either.*'

'My partner did,' said Paul.

'She was losing. But in the terms of the We, you were being justified.'

'No!' Paul jumped up. 'You do not say that!' he shouted. 'You do not say that!'

'Don't I?' said Lewis, without blinking. 'I think I do.'

'You are wrong!'

'You are offended.'

'Yes!'

'Good. The deeper the offence, Paul, the closer we get. Sit down. I am not doing this because I like to hurt you.'

Grimly, Paul sat.

'Remember,' said Lewis. 'Everything that's happened to you has also happened to each of us. We had lives back there, networks we lived in. We were pulled out, like you. Me to manage this station, May to be its doctor and Van to study that giant up there and— Hah! To look for life on the coldest object in the solar system! Paul, doesn't it strike you as . . . *strange* that so much of the effort of this station is devoted to ST2? Fifty per cent, indeed, since you and May and I are only here to support the functions of Vandamme?'

'No. That is standard.'

'But *why* is it standard? Whatever the mission and whatever the conditions? It is standard because it is important to the We. Alien life? Here? Come off it! But still it is standard. The We knows it is missing something. Locked in its make-up is the idea of social interaction, which it inherits from the individuals that compose it. Social interaction has been the key to the growth of the human brain, both through the generations and to the learning child. The We has a complex environment – think of all the adjustments and balances necessary to maintain a stable world and climate back there – but it has no one to interact with. It may be dimly aware of a range of possible actions, from mating to murder and conquest. But it is alone. There is only one of it. There only ever will be. It is a new-born, wailing in a dark room with no one to hear.'

Behind his shoulder an image changed. It showed a man on Earth, painting a portrait of a woman who sat naked and smiling before him. The man had a long beard and wore robes from another time. Between his plump forefinger and thumb a fine brush caressed the canvas as if it were the woman's bare skin.

Paul brought his eyes back to Lewis's face. 'I think you are lying,' he said.

Lewis's brows thickened on his forehead. 'Lying? Why would I lie to you? I am not lying, Paul!'

'You said humans are not human any more. That is not the truth.'

'I may have simplified for effect.'

'You lied.'

'I did not lie. I told the truth.'

'It is not the truth if you simplify things.'

'Yes, it *damned* well is!' Lewis leaned forward until his head filled Paul's vision. His face was redder than Paul had ever seen it. Paul felt the unfamiliar stir of physical anxiety.

'Paul – you want a purpose. I know that. You think it's to work our communications for the We. You still want to be part of the We, even though you are cut off from it. That's what you think will make your existence bearable. And I'm sorry for you. But let me ask you this. *Why man this station at all?*'

'To learn!' said Paul.

'To learn what? What is there here that a machine could not measure and report back to Earth by itself?'

Paul opened his mouth to answer. The answer seemed immediate. It was there. But . . .

To learn what?

The station had to be manned. He had known that all along. Everyone he had worked with had known it.

But when he searched his brain he found nothing. Only the incidental advantages – the reduced turnaround times for tests and experiments, the increased capacity for self-repair, the superiority of human pattern-recognition – presented themselves. They were true but inadequate. Nothing substantial answered.

Still he searched, as if in a nightmare, opening door after door in his mind behind which the great facts should have been stored, and still there was nothing. The walls of his mind trembled and its floor seemed to drop open and pitch him into stomach-dropping darkness. And the eyes of Lewis watched him all the time.

'It's bad, isn't it?' said Lewis. 'When you see that we add a vast cost, and almost no value, to what robots could do here in our place. Where's the sense in that?'

Paul looked at his hands, thin and brittle and bony at the end of his brittle and bony limbs.

'It makes no sense because you are trying to understand it at the level of *individual* intellect. But the We is not an individual. It is regressive, inconsiderate of its parts, childishly selfish for the whole. You and I are just tiny extensions of itself. It perceives us no more than the ant's nest perceives the ant. But when you add up all the little messages flickering around inside it, you come up with one tendency. A blind and basic instinct. Come on, Paul. What activity in nature demands the greatest effort – an effort that sometimes seems vastly in excess of that necessary to secure a return?'

Paul stirred. Then he said hoarsely: 'Making . . . children.'

'Making children. Reproduction. Exactly. The We is trying to reproduce.'

Paul could only stare at him.

'The We is trying to reproduce, Paul. It is driven by its genes – *our* genes, which first made our brains and have now made the We. Genes don't think. They feel, blindly. They try out everything – anything they can to give the next genera- tion a better chance. What are a few losses? We're all expendable. So the We is feeling out into space. It finds a crevice and, however unpromising it may be, it plants a seed there. Four hundred people went to Mars. For Titan it was fifty. Here it was just four. Given the distance and the conditions, it's a wonder that it was thought worth any. But it was possible, and because it was possible, Earth just couldn't leave it alone. So here we are – us and the other eleven stations dotted around the solar system, all struggling with our different challenges. The We does not care which lasts and which does not, as long as some do. That space escalator that's been built. Did you see it?'

Paul heard himself say, 'I was asleep.'

'That thing! Can you imagine what it cost to put up? And it won't make the life of a single human any better. It can't. But with it, Earth can build ships far more massive than could ever be kicked up out of its gravity. Why must they be so massive? To shield our genetic material from the effects of the solar wind. I checked the specs of the craft that brought you here, Paul. You went waltzing with the Sun itself and I'll bet you didn't absorb a single particle. That elevator – it's just a damned great dick. And with it the We is trying to fertilize the galaxy!'

'But . . . we cannot breed here!'

Lewis looked at him.

'It is crazy!' Paul protested. 'In this place – the gravity . . . Crazy!'

'That,' said Lewis, turning away, 'is what I have said to Earth.'

He rested on his toes with his hands behind his back. He seemed to be watching an image on the wall, of a yellow stone building with ornate towers standing under a hard blue sky. A place where men had worshipped their god.

'I received a query, about three years after we arrived here,' said Lewis. 'I think that was when I really started to understand what was going on. Anyway, I sent a reply assessing the environment, the risk factors, the constraints . . . Basically I told Earth to forget it. You were already on your way, of course, but since then Earth has rather lost interest in us. Frankly I can't say I'm sorry. The least it can do for us now is leave us alone.'

Paul looked at him looking at the image on the wall.

'So here we are,' said Lewis. 'The four of us. The last humans. Maybe the last ever. What are we going to do about that, Paul?'

Paul's eyes narrowed. 'Do you believe in God?'

Lewis snorted. 'God no! Why do you ask?'

'Vandamme said I should. I thought you all did.'

'And you think that if I believe in God then I will believe anything. I've paid a great price to recover my mind, Paul. The last thing I'm going to do is enslave it to something else. But . . . I can see why Van does. She has to believe in something. We all have to. If we didn't, we would all go mad.'

'What do you believe in?'

'The future, Paul. What else?'

'The future – for us?'

'There's always a future! As long as we're not alone. And I'm not. Neither are you, Paul.'

'What do you mean?'

'I don't have to spell it out for you, do I?'

Paul glared at him. 'I believe in *work*,' he said. And he left the chamber.

VII

He dreamed of an open window, with warm air flowing in. Outside the sun was bright, but softened to a kindly glow by the protecting veils of atmosphere. He could hear birdsong and the branches of trees moving. He heard it all very clearly, as he had rarely heard it in his waking mind. The world was full of colours.

He could feel nothing through his World Ear. He did not have one. But soon he would. They were coming to fit him with it. They were coming to open his mind to all the minds around him again. Knowing that brought a glow like the sun. He would be safe, surrounded by all the mental chatter in which he belonged. He would know he had a purpose that served them all.

They would come soon. *She* was bringing them to him, leading them up the walkways and along the passages to his door. Soon it would open. He waited, looking at the door.

He was looking out of the window at the city. He was looking at the high buildings and the low buildings, at the lines of trees and the bubbles nestling among them. He was looking for Her, coming towards him with the boy beside her. He was looking for anyone moving towards him along the avenues, coming to him, knowing he was there, even though it would take them a long time to reach him. But he could see no one. He waited. Still he saw no one.

And he knew that the building around him was empty. The city was empty. There was no one there. There was no one left on Earth.

He woke, in the station.

It was eerie, stepping through the airlock. He entered a common room exactly like the one he had just left, with a curving ceiling, cream-lit walls and the doors of four work-chambers, a kitchen and a sanitary unit spaced evenly down the sides. It was as if he had turned round without noticing, so that when leaving the airlock he had arrived back at the point from which he had entered it.

This was the Alfa suite – the original living–quarter module that the crew had inhabited when they had first arrived on the station. It was heated, pressurized and powered to the same standards as the living-quarter module Paul had just left. Only Lewis would know what the extra drain on the station's resources must be.

The station was designed for two couples. Each pair of

work-chambers had just one two-person sleeping chamber associated with it. But because Paul and Vandamme were not a couple the crew needed extra space. Therefore, shortly before Paul's arrival, they had opened up the Bravo suite, one of three additional living-quarter modules that had been provided for redundancy in case of impact or other damage. May and Lewis had moved into the Bravo suite because of growing problems with the ageing systems in Alfa. It was in the Bravo suite that Paul had woken, and it was the Bravo suite that he now inhabited with May and Lewis. Vandamme remained in Alfa, alone.

Three of the seals to the work-chambers were open. The walls of the rooms inside were blank and the equipment stowed away. The door to the fourth chamber was closed. He stopped outside it and called. No one answered. He went in anyway.

He came to rest on the moon's surface.

The wall-display showed a 360-degree view of the landscape, taken from one of the search crawlers operating outside the station. The gas giant, half in shadow, hung in the blackness overhead. The stars were bright and did not twinkle. It was as if Paul had stepped out of the station altogether. Around him, glowing an eerie purple in the blue twilight, was the ice.

It was everywhere. It heaved in great waves like a frozen

sea: low curves and sharp ridges, remnants of ancient flows. Close to, the shapes were fantastic. There were ripples and curls, eddies and spills, and spines erupting from them like the fins of vast sea-creatures in a nightmare ocean. Tiny frost particles drifted, carried on the thinnest of winds. On the horizon a line of icy geysers lifted their fumes to the sky. Everything else was still.

To his right, a kilometre away, was a dark streak that might be the lip of a chasm such as the station nestled in. But there must be thousands of such chasms. He could not see Thorsten's pylon or any of the Sun mirrors or radio transmitters. Nor could he recognize any of the natural features that populated the landscape around the home canyon – not 'Chesapeake', not 'Macclesfield', not even the high, triangular point of 'Humperdinck', which was almost always in view. They might have been just out of sight beyond a nearby ridge of ice.

Vandamme was sitting at her console in the middle of that barren, deathly landscape. She was punching a command into the keyboard, patiently pressing one key after another. The pointer was at her elbow, unused. She had not looked up when Paul entered.

Paul took a skip across the chamber. 'Do you mind if I join you?'

Vandamme lifted her head from the keyboard and looked

at the wall. The working screen was focused on a patch of surface ice. Probing into the picture was an arm of the crawler. It had driven into the ice and seemed to be turning slowly. It must have just begun drilling.

'No,' said Vandamme. 'I don't mind.'

She had not taken her eyes off the display. She was watching the drilling arm intently, as if she expected to have to intervene with another command at any moment. And she might. That drill would be working in a temperature of some thirty degrees Kelvin. If it had been hardened steel it would have shattered like glass.

The waste of ice all around him; the woman at the console; and the image of the robot arm on the bubble wall.

'Boring for life forms?' asked Paul.

He heard the double meaning in his words even as he spoke them. But Vandamme answered the question he had intended.

'For signs of extinct life. Yes.'

'Have you found any?'

'Not yet.'

Not after ten years of searching.

'And . . . conditions to support life?'

'There is water.'

'But too cold, surely.'

Vandamme looked up. Not at Paul but at the half-disc of the giant planet overhead.

'The orbit is retrograde,' she said. 'So the moon may have been captured at a late stage in the formation of the solar system. We do not know its previous history.'

Paul looked up too. Then he looked around at the bizarre shapes of ice again. 'Where are we?'

'In my chamber,' said Vandamme, without any trace of humour. Her eyes were fixed on the monitor once more.

Paul tried again. 'How far is the crawler from the station?'

'One hundred and twenty-three kilometres.'

No wonder the display showed nothing that Paul recognized. And if he stayed here in Vandamme's chamber he could watch the scenery change as the crawlers lumbered on across the moon's surface. The scene would change and change and change, and yet like a dream it would always be the same.

'How many bores have you drilled?' he asked. 'Approximately?'

'Approximately ten thousand,' said Vandamme.

Paul thought that if he had asked for an exact figure she would have given him one. Ten thousand boreholes meant a thousand boreholes a year. Say three a day, day in, day out. And no life, nor any sign that there had ever been life, out here. This was ST2 – the long, meticulous, pointless search.

Turning over every pebble on a beach that ran on for ever.

There was nowhere to sit. Paul stood with his hands on his hips just inside the chamber seal. He watched the woman at her console desk, surrounded by images of wasteland.

To his surprise, he found that she was no longer so difficult to look at. Her head was tilted towards him as she worked. The most prominent features were her eyebrows, a clean arc, and the neat curves of her cheek and chin. The strange proportions of her head and limbs did not seem so strange now. She was another human, out here with him.

She was ignoring him. But she was not being rude. She was just being herself. She was giving her attention to the thing that she felt had priority – her work. Her ten thousandth borehole which, like all its predecessors, would show no sign that life had ever existed in this place.

Of course it would not. Not in all the probes and explorations man had attempted within the solar system had they found the merest single-celled organism that had not proved to be an infection from Earth. And still the search went on, obsessively. After this hole, Vandamme would move the crawler and make another. And another after that. *Boring for life?* That would have been a joke, if only Paul had intended it.

Click, went the keyboard under Vandamme's forefinger. *Click, click, click.* On the monitor, the drilling arm stopped.

'Do you think we will find life here?' Paul asked carefully.

'It is possible. There is a liquid water mantle, deep down.'

'But intelligent life?'

Vandamme frowned at the chamber wall, as though the thought was relevant but strange. 'No, of course not,' she said.

'There must be some, somewhere.'

'Perhaps. But it is not close. We have been scanning space for a hundred years. We have seen nothing yet that we could confirm to be an intelligent transmission. If it takes a hundred years for their transmissions to reach us, then it would be two hundred years before they could receive our replies.'

'Perhaps they are closer but we have not yet developed the right technology.'

'The technology is adequate.'

'Then perhaps they are hiding from us. Hiding in the shadows.' The image in his mind, of faraway beings cowering in the recesses of space and peering nervously towards Earth's system, brought a grim smile to his lips.

Vandamme took it seriously. 'They would have to have been aware of us before we began to listen for them – before our first radio telescopes were constructed.'

'You think that impossible?'

'Anything is possible, but it is not likely,' said the woman who hunted for life in the coldest places of the solar system.

'Will not alien life be so alien that we will not know if it is life?'

Now Paul was nudging the conversation in the direction he wanted it to go. He did not want to talk about alien life. He did not want to talk about the magnetic field or the radio. He wanted to talk about Earth. But he feared that if he asked her directly, she might lie, and he would not know if she had lied. So he was choosing his questions as carefully as he could.

He was also having to search for the right words. For the first time since arriving at the station he was the one who was proposing ideas. And although his speech had improved faster than he could have imagined, he was still severely limited by what he knew how to say. *We will not know if it is life* fell far short of describing the debates that would seethe through the World Ear networks, perhaps for years, if evidence of alien organisms were ever to be found.

'All life shares four characteristics,' said Vandamme, as if reciting a lesson. 'It uses energy. It adapts. It replicates itself. And it tends towards complexity.'

'If an alien looked at humans on Earth,' said Paul, 'would it see many creatures? Or would it see one, composed of many things all linked together by the World Ear?'

'It would depend upon the nature of the alien,' said Vandamme.

'But what do you think?'

Vandamme was silent. So Paul prompted gently: 'When you look at Earth, what do you think?'

Her head jerked away from the screen. Her fingers left the keyboard.

After a moment she said, 'I try not to.' She began to tap laboriously at her keyboard again. Paul watched her.

It would depend upon the nature of the alien. If the alien were one of a race of individuals, it would see first the individuals. But if it were itself a composite creature, sharing its consciousness among its organisms, there might be something else for it to see.

Paul could accept that. It was less extreme than Lewis's vision of a single brain. It simply said that a human could be both an individual and at the same time a component of something greater. That had always been so. That could be true for almost any form of life.

So did it mean anything at all?

Where did the consciousness rest? Could there be an 'I' and a 'We' at the same time? And which ruled which?

It would depend upon the nature of the alien. A clever, elusive answer. It did not address the real question. Had she meant to be clever and elusive? Paul did not know. But she was familiar with the idea that the human race might have fused into a single consciousness. She had not found it strange when Paul had suggested it to her. Did she think it was true?

I try not to.

Suddenly Vandamme spoke. 'What is it like, having the World Ear these days?'

What was it like? thought Paul.

The image that came was of his partner, sitting on the end of the bed in the room that overlooked the sea. It had been a bright morning, with the sunlight pouring in so strongly that the wall-displays seemed dull. He had just shown her the plan that would take him away to the station. She was not looking at him. She was looking at the floor with her face furrowed. She was not crying and she never would. Already the rising stress in her body had triggered the therapy routines she relied on. The images she sent back were dark and fragmented. He saw, rather than received, her sense of loss and bewilderment: the sudden, gaping un-certainty of a future without him; her fears for the child who would know no father. For him it had not outweighed the immense force of the proposal from headquarters, with all its myriad ramifications reaching out through medical, engineering and astronomical networks. But it could not be blotted out either. It was there, a small, sad coda to the great thing he carried in his brain.

His throat was dry. 'You belong,' he said.

Click, click, click. More slow commands, relayed to the crawler on the unimaginable cold of the moon surface, a hundred and twenty-three kilometres away.

'Do you have any problems with your transmissions?' said Paul.

'No.'

'Never any interference between you and the crawlers?'

'No.'

'What about the data you send to Earth?'

'The transmission window is not affected.'

'Thank you.'

There was a message from Earth waiting for him when he returned to his chamber.

His signal recording the passage of the tail had been corrupted. He was to investigate the cause and report.

VIII

'Paul?'

It was May's voice, calling from just outside his work-chamber. He did not answer.

'Paul, are you all right?'

'Yes. I am all right.'

There was a hesitation. Then: 'May I come in?'

He thought about it for a moment.

'Yes.'

She entered and came to rest beside him as he sat at his workstation. 'Paul, is something the matter?' she asked. 'Lewis and I were expecting you at supper.'

'I ate here.'

'You should have said. We were worried about you.'

Paul shrugged. He had known they would worry. He had not cared much because he had been angry. He was still angry.

'It's better to eat together, Paul,' said May. 'It may seem old-fashioned to you but it helps to keep us friends.'

Paul scowled. 'I am busy,' he said.

May peered at the figures on his console. 'It's long past the end of your shift. What's the crisis?'

'Our transmissions of the passage of the tail were corrupted.'

'But that keeps happening, Paul! It's not like it was the first time.'

'This is the first time it has happened to me.'

'You're upset,' she said, 'and tired. You can't be working efficiently any more. Wouldn't it be better to take a rest?'

'Not until I can find out how it happened.'

He had monitored the transmissions himself. He had sent that test signal and received an acknowledgement from Earth. He had checked the downloads and the modulation. He had double-checked, because he had known that he was agitated after his talk with Lewis, and therefore he might have made mistakes. There had been no mistakes. He had watched the first groups go out. The automatic acknowledgements had come back from Earth on cue, eight hours later. There had been no sign that anything had been wrong. And now there was this.

Your 25:03:0141: Message corrupted. The following groups unreadable . . .
. . . Investigate and report.

It might have been a fault affecting the station transmitters. The two auxiliaries, working together, were powerful enough to have jammed a signal from the main transmitter if they had somehow fired at the same time. But the records showed nothing. They were clean. He had also checked the main transmitter files, in case it had somehow resumed transmissions after the signal had been sent, confusing the satellite relay to Earth. Now he was hunting through all the files of allied operations (control signals to crawlers, automatic activations of arrays, even the pressure readings from the external bubble layers) to see if there was anything that might inadvertently have bled across to affect the message, perhaps by corrupting the modulation of the data onto the signal in a way that he had not noticed. He was finding nothing.

He *should* be able to find it. It *should* be within his capabilities. That was what he had been trained for. That was what he had been sent here for. But one by one the possibilities were being eliminated. He was angry. Angry because he could not find it. When May peered past him at the screen he felt resentment prickle around his neck and shoulders.

After a moment she said, 'We're worried about you, Paul.'

'Why?'

'We think you're finding it tough.'

'I will get used to it,' he said.

'Yeah. But you've hit a crisis and you're trying to cope alone. You can't do that. You need us to help you along. We need you to be part of us anyway. You'll need us much more. You will.'

'You stay in your room when you want.'

'Not like this.'

'I will do my shifts. I will keep to the rules. But when I am not on my shift I will be where I want. What is the matter?'

'The *matter*, Paul, is that you're having to make a massive adjustment! You came here trusting the We, like the rest of us. You've been utterly, utterly betrayed. Either you don't see it yet, or you do but don't want to believe it. The longer it takes, the worse it'll be for you. You'll chase round and round in smaller circles, trying to find something that isn't there—'

'It is there,' he snapped. 'I will find it.'

'Thorsten couldn't,' she said.

She spoke softly. But as she looked at him her face hardened. Paul realized he was glaring at her. He reset his face muscles.

'You think because I shut my door that I will—'

'I'm not saying that, Paul. Please – I'm just saying—'

'You think I don't know about people who kill

110

themselves. You think it has not happened on Earth. You are wrong. It *has* happened. I remember. There was a man who did it. He did it because he had been cut off. No one would connect with him. They would not connect with him because they knew he had lied.'

.He said the word *lied* with emphasis, deliberately. But if May understood, she did not show it.

'I don't mean you'll do what Thorsten did . . .'

'I do not know what he did.'

'. . . that's not what I'm trying to say . . .'

Anger rose in Paul like vomit. 'Why do you *hide*?' he yelled.

She stared at him, shocked. Her eyes went to the door. He thought she would get up and leave him. She wanted to, but she did not. She took a big breath.

'You want me to tell you about Thorsten,' she said.

'Lewis said he would brief me. He has not. *Why* has he not briefed me?'

'For God's sake, Paul! Why are you so suspicious? There've been a million and one things to do with your induction . . . Look, what do you want to know?'

'What happened.'

'But we've *told* you . . . Oh, all right. It's all logged, but – but I suppose that doesn't really make it real.'

She looked at her hands, then drew another breath.

'He was working on the loss of transmissions, like you. He had decided it was the field, by then, but he couldn't see . . . Anyway, he stopped observing the schedules. He'd work in a kind of frenzy, for hours at a burst. And then he'd do nothing, not even when it was his watch. We didn't think very much of it to begin with. We all had stuff we were trying to cope with. But that was the start. We let him get into habits that weren't good for him. And by the time we did worry it was too late. He wasn't responding even to Van. Then, one watch, he put on a pressure suit and went into the outer layers . . .

'He wasn't supposed to. The rule is that you don't go out of the habitable bubbles without alerting the rest of us. The first I knew was when Lewis called us into his work-chamber. He had Thorsten on his monitor. Thorsten had gone right out into the radiation layers, where the gas isn't for breathing but for shielding, and is cold and dense like mist. Lewis was arguing with him over the intercom. There was something odd about Thorsten's answers – not evasive, just uncaring. I remember feeling suddenly that I didn't know what was going to happen next. Then Lewis got Van to try. She bent over the speaker and said, "Thorsten?" And he just said, "Goodbye, Erin." There was an awful hissing. I looked at the microphone and I thought, What's wrong with it? Then I realized he had opened the seals on his pressure suit.'

She had put her hand to her cheek. She looked away, remembering.

'He asphyxiated before we could reach him. And suddenly we were only three.'

'You went out to him?'

For a moment she did not seem to have heard him. She was reliving the moments she had described. Then, slowly, she said, 'Lewis did. Of course we shouldn't have let him do it alone. But none of us were thinking clearly. I suppose he wanted to spare us dealing with the body. That was the worst. Waiting for him to come back, thinking that he was out there, alone, where Thorsten had just done what he had done . . . I think it was the most horrible moment of my life. When something like that has happened, it just seems the most likely thing in the world that it's going to happen again . . .'

After a moment she said, 'But he did come back. And then he got us all going again, just as he had at the beginning when we arrived, all sick and lost, and saw for the first time what it was going to be like. He's brilliant, in some ways. In others he drives me mad. And so does Van. God – the things I could do to Van sometimes! Was it *my* fault she lost Thorsten? And now she goes work, pray, work, pray, and nothing else! We've got to get her to come *out*! I thought she would, now you're here. The four of us—' She checked herself.

'We have to be like . . . like family. Because we're all we have. You see?'

'Yes,' he said. 'I see.'

He said, 'You are saying that I should not look for the fault, because it is the field and I can do nothing about that. You are saying that I should rest, take meals with you and learn to be as humans were before the World Ear. You are saying that if I do not do this I will become depressed, as Thorsten did.'

She was still for a moment. Then she nodded and said, 'Yes. Well done. That's it in a nutshell. That's exactly what I'm saying.'

'Nutshell? There are no nuts here.'

'Not that kind of nut,' she said. Then she laughed – a short, shrill laugh as if she were close to tears. 'Oh God! Of course words don't get used like that on Earth any more! Why use words to make an image when you can send diagrams and pictures and stuff? Oh God! Sometimes I feel so . . . *left behind.*'

She sighed. Her eyes were on the floor.

Paul looked at the floor too. He thought of the thin fabrics that supported them in these little warm bubbles, suspended just a short distance above the surface where nitrogen froze and the ice was four hundred kilometres thick.

'What do you believe in?' he said.

'Believe?'

'Lewis says you must believe.'

She looked up. There was a slight, secret smile on her face.

'I believe in wonderful things, Paul. For all of us. And they're going to happen.'

'What things?'

'Oh – all sorts. Some are really, really important. Others aren't, but I can still believe in them. Right now I believe you should get some rest. And when you're feeling better I think you should go down to Van and have a really good long talk about the field. Get into those ions and flows and things that you both know about. She'll love that. You should do it every day. It'll be good for both of you.

'And I promise you, Paul. It *does* get better. When I think back to how we were when we first arrived and saw what it was going to be like . . . we all wept. Even Lewis. Even Van. We'd all get together and hug each other for long, long minutes. It really helps. Do you want a hug, Paul?'

She held her arms out to him. Her eyes were liquid. His heart bumped as if the floor had suddenly shifted under his feet.

'No, thank you,' he said.

Her face went blank. 'All right. Be tough if you want. I'll

go and find Lewis and hug him all I like. But tell me you're feeling better.'

'I am feeling better.'

Another pause. She was waiting for something more. But he did not want to give it to her.

'All right then,' she said. 'Goodnight, Paul. Don't work too hard.'

She left. The seal closed behind her.

That's it in a nutshell.

That was it in a lie.

They wanted him to think it was the field. It could not be the field.

If it had been the field causing discharges on the satellite, it would have shut down everything that depended on the radio. It would have confused Vandamme's link with her crawlers, scattered far out across the ice. But the crawlers had experienced no interference – not once in ten years. Vandamme had confirmed that. Whether she had meant to or not, she had destroyed that theory in a sentence. For the crawlers at least, the radio had always worked as it should.

So had the satellite. He still had to check the satellite's Earthbound antenna but it would not be that. A fault on the satellite would not make the crew lie.

I don't have to spell it out for you, do I? No. Not any more.

116

He understood it now. They wanted him here, but not because he was a telemetrist. They wanted him here because of the woman who shut herself away beyond the airlock door.

The four of us . . .

May was dreaming of 'wonderful things' that were going to happen. What happened between a man and woman? *Do you know, I've no idea!* Lewis had said. And, *I'm looking forward to—* And then he had stopped himself. To what? To something new. Something that had not happened in the station before – and that Lewis had told Earth could never happen.

What are we going to do about that, Paul?

Alone in his chamber, Paul guessed it. He guessed too that the interference with the signals was part of it. As May had said, he had been utterly betrayed.

It had been done deliberately. To get him here.

He sent to Earth for a Hunter.

IX

If a single human was an axon in the brain of a larger consciousness, then a Hunter was a white blood cell. It was a program designed to identify and destroy electronic threats that had invaded where they should not have done. And because a Hunter was no more than a mass of electronic coding, it could be fired through space at the speed of light.

When it came, two days later, he showed it to May. He showed it to her because he wanted her to see, without understanding, that he had the power to destroy her. With the Hunter he could strip away the lies of which the station was made.

May was thrilled.

She jumped lightly up and down in his work-chamber, clapping her hands. 'Hey, Lewis!' she called. 'Hey, come and see what Paul has got! You come and see!' And then, as Lewis drifted in through the seal, she said. 'Show it again, Paul. From the beginning!'

Paul clicked the manual controls. Cold, concealed rage

drove his movements and made them deliberate. There was no hurry. He had the rest of his life for what he was going to do.

'Watch!' said May.

The working area of the bubble wall blinked and changed. It showed a scene from four and a half billion kilometres away and perhaps a million years ago – a level land of tall yellow grasses, dotted with curiously shaped trees, sunlit under a hard blue sky.

'Can you make it three-sixty, Paul?' asked May.

Wooden-faced, he clicked his controls again. Now the scene filled the whole of the chamber wall, all around them, so that but for the tasteless air and the few square metres of grey floor they might have been standing on that plain themselves. Lewis, coming to rest inside the chamber, appeared to have ducked under the branch of a fat-trunked tree that spread its dark green shade behind him.

'What's the excitement?' he asked.

'Ssh! Call it, Paul. It's wonderful!'

'Hunter,' Paul said.

At once the yellow grasses parted and a creature stepped heavily out. It was a man, or very nearly. It was the same height as Paul and Lewis, with an intelligent, ape-like face under a high domed skull and heavy ridges above the eyes. Its body too was man-like, but thickset and heavy, with far

119

too much muscle in the arm and neck and thigh. It was naked, dark-skinned, and as it stumped towards them they could see that it was covered with fine dark hair that thickened into a mat on its head, on the back of its neck and in the indistinct region of its groin.

'Very discreet,' said Lewis.

'Wouldn't have bothered me,' said May smugly. 'I'm a doctor, remember?'

'And your diagnosis, Doctor?'

'I'd say the poor guy's missing something.'

The creature halted, appearing to watch them. In one hand it held a long sharpened stick like a spear, sinister in its slenderness.

'It's a Hunter, is it, Paul?' said Lewis.

'Yes,' Paul said. 'To help me find the communications fault.'

He used the word *fault*, although in his mind he meant *culprit*. Lewis nodded slowly.

'Thorsten had one of those, once,' said May. 'But it didn't look like this, did it? What happened to it?'

'I cleared it out with a lot of other data a few years ago,' said Lewis. 'A shame, really. I was in one of my puritanical moods. I don't suppose this one—' He broke off, watching the creature thoughtfully.

Suddenly he put one foot forward, lifted a palm towards

the screen and declaimed in a loud, dramatic voice, 'Come away, servant, come! I am ready now. Approach, my Ariel; come!'

The mouth of the ape-man moved. A voice rich in resonance answered, '*All hail, great master! Grave sir, hail! I come to answer thy best pleasure; be't to fly, to swim, to—*'

'It does! That's wonderful!' said Lewis, smiling. And then, striking another pose, he chanted in a quick, light voice, '*Leporello, ove sei?*'

'*Son qui, per mia disgrazia, e voi?*' fluted the ape-man.

'*Son qui,*' put in Lewis.

'*Chi è morto—*' began the Hunter.

But again Lewis interrupted. 'No one's dead, thank you very much.' He turned to the others. 'Amazing what they get loaded with. It's as if the works themselves know they are on the verge of extinction, so they hide in every corner they can in an effort to survive. What was once immortal art is now useless electronic clutter in programs primarily intended for cleaning up computer systems.'

'I remember that. That was *opera*, wasn't it?' said May.

'Part of one. But you're nearly twenty years out of date. Opera doesn't happen back there any more. Stories about people – individuals – are dying out. Celebrity gossip is confined to the less developed networks. Imagination is less and less concerned with alternative individual existences.

Abstract audio-visual experience is becoming the dominant art form.'

'Not just audio-visual,' said Paul. 'Most forms are for smell and touch too.'

'And taste as well?'

'Sometimes.'

'Clever, isn't it?' said May, still beaming at the ape-man. 'What else does it know?'

'Hunter,' said Lewis. 'What is the age of the Earth?'

'*Four point five billion years*,' said the Hunter, in a round smooth voice unlike either it had used so far.

'And what is the mass of the Sun?'

'*One point nine nine times ten to the power of thirty kilograms*.'

'How do you know this?'

'*I have applied the rules of physics to observation*.'

'And what if your rules are wrong?' said Lewis with a wicked smile.

The ape-man looked at them blankly.

'What if they are wrong, Hunter?'

'It can't answer that,' Paul snapped.

'Of course it can't. If May had asked, "What else is it loaded with?" the answer would be more than any of us have time to find out. Just like the human chromosome, ninety per cent of which contains information that is never activated. It will have AI capabilities, some pattern recognition and the capacity to learn. But it can't think like a human. What I've done is ask it to question its original programming. It can't do that. Don't be fooled by its appearance. A walking, talking ape-man from a past age is exactly what it isn't.'

His eyes lingered on the ape-man figure, which watched them impassively.

'*Homo Erectus*,' he murmured. 'Our probable ancestor. Why do you suppose it was made to look like that, Paul?'

'I don't know,' said Paul stiffly. 'I only asked for one that worked with speech.'

'And we were sent a face from a million years ago. So speech isn't just history. It's gone into the fossil record.'

'Is that what they're telling us?' gasped May. 'God, that's rude!'

'Have you seen enough?' said Paul. And when no one answered he said, 'Proceed, Hunter.'

The Hunter turned and walked heavily away into the sunlit grasses. Lewis watched it go, rubbing his chin softly with one hand. 'A Hunter,' he murmured. 'Well, well.'

'You said Thorsten had one,' said Paul.

Lewis looked at him. Paul could not read his eyes. 'Yes. It didn't find anything.'

'This one will be more capable,' said Paul.

'Oh, I should think so,' said Lewis.

'Why did you delete Thorsten's?'

'Because . . .' said Lewis with a tight, secret smile, 'because I was wasting far too much time playing with it. Well, thank you, Paul, for showing this to us. Best of luck with it. When you're not using it, perhaps you'd turn it over to me and we'll see if it knows any duets.'

'Shit!' said May, following him out of the chamber. 'Must I put up with you singing as well as snoring now?'

'I promise I won't sing in my sleep. Where's Van? That thing's probably carrying all the scripture that was ever written. Shall I tell her, do you think?'

'She's hiding, I guess. And you know damned well she won't take any help from a thing like that . . .'

When they had gone, Paul muttered aloud, 'Stupid!'

He meant himself. Lewis would know that Hunters were for malicious programs. He would wonder why Paul had not said so. And the answer would be obvious: because Paul thought that one of them might be the author of whatever was affecting the communications. Lewis would have guessed that. And he had said nothing.

Stupid! It had been stupid to show it to May! And he knew why he had done it – because he was angry. Anger was making him stupid.

He turned to his controls, meaning to reset the displays.

To his surprise he saw that the Hunter was back, looking at him from the wall of his chamber, even though Paul had seen it walk into the long, pale grasses only moments before.

And now he realized that the creature was not exaggeratedly thickset and heavy, as it had first seemed. Its muscular neck and limbs were no more than a man would need to support his frame in the gravity of Earth. To the Earthbound eye the creature might even have seemed graceful. But his own had adjusted to the physiques of the station and the way that a body moved in low gravity. It no longer saw his companions as hideous. It saw Earth-things as fat and ungainly. Even the meaning of beauty had changed up here.

'I said, proceed, Hunter,' he repeated.

'*I have finished*,' said Hunter.

'Finished? Already?'

'*I have searched all the local systems.*'

'And?'

'*There is nothing.*'

Paul's hands dropped to his sides. 'What do you mean, "nothing"?'

'*There is nothing.*'

'You have found no irregular entries affecting the radio communications?'

'*There are many entries that do not conform to the*

125

required standards. I have assessed all of them. They are benign.'

Paul fell slowly into his chair. He put his fist to his mouth. After a moment he bit it, hard enough for it to hurt.

'Keep looking,' he said. 'Look for different things. Look for anything that might be intelligent interference with the radio communications.'

'Define "intelligent" for this purpose.'

Paul thought.

'It can see something, react, see what happens and learn to do better,' he said.

'I have already applied this parameter.'

So the Hunter had conducted its search, found nothing, and reset its criteria automatically before trying again – and all in the time it had taken for Lewis and May to leave his chamber.

It was indeed capable. And it had still found nothing.

'There will be something,' said Paul. 'Try again.'

Wordlessly the Hunter stomped off into the grasses.

X

The display reflected inside his pressure-suit helmet included a temperature reading. It stood at minus eighty degrees Celsius: as cold as an Antarctic winter. The exterior pressure was about one half of an atmosphere. He was standing within fifty metres of the living quarters.

Vandamme was taking him on his first tour of the outer layers of the station. According to the schedules, it should have been her rest period. But Lewis had found some reason to shuffle the watches, and when he looked at them again he had said that Paul's companion must be Vandamme. Paul had not been surprised.

Her face was invisible inside her helmet. Her voice, however, came over the intercom as clearly as if they had been back in the living quarters together. Her words were clipped and dry. He wondered if she knew why Lewis had chosen her for this. It infuriated him that she might know, and that even so she could be so passionless. But his anger was not at her. It was aimed at May and Lewis. Of the three of them now, Vandamme was indeed the most tolerable.

'This is the hangar for the mobile equipment,' she was saying. 'Surface crawlers and harvesters, mostly. The crawlers are of three types, Search, Construction and Utility. Searchers are for ST2. Constructors were used to erect the station and will do the repairs if we have an impact. Utilities do everything else.'

The hangar was a great grey bubble, far larger than the main living-quarter chamber. The curving roof rose to three times the height of Paul's head. Ranked down the centre of it were lines of crawlers, each two to three metres long and roughly a metre high. Their wheels were big, set so wide that their wheel-base must have been almost square. The bodies were brightly coloured, so that they would be visible on the moon's landscape if it were ever necessary to search for them by sight. The utility and construction crawlers were yellow, angular machines with small solar packs and numerous limbs folded up together like the legs of ungainly spiders. The searchers were orange. These were meaner-looking things, with a high clearance and even wider axles than the utilities. They had big wheels that rose above their bodies, long antennae and large solar packs to give them range.

Compared with these, the grey colour of the harvesters made them almost invisible where they stood in a line against the near wall. They were smaller than the crawlers, with less pronounced wheel-bases, little wheels and long limbs. Even so, they too had the same low, wide-splayed look of machines that must keep their stability in low gravity.

'Shouldn't they be working?' asked Paul.

'They are. The ones you see here are the spares. There's a three hundred per cent redundancy in case of failures – or an impact.'

'Three hundred per cent?'

'That's standard across the station, but it varies from case to case. Much of our instrumentation and computing power is in the outer layers, where the natural temperature is low enough to permit superconductivity. Of course that means the sites are hardest to get at and most at risk from impact. So the redundancy is not less than five hundred per cent. On the other hand – you see that?'

Synchronized with her words in his ear, the arm of the suited figure beside him pointed. At the far end of the hangar was another crawler, far larger than the others and coloured red. They skipped down the central aisle towards it. Close to, it seemed enormous. Its eight wheels rose higher than Paul's head. Its body was fat and featureless. It carried no solar packs. At either end it had a cluster of limbs, but these were no more and no larger than those of the utility crawlers. They seemed ridiculously small for such a bloated thing.

'We landed with three of those. Almost the first thing we found was that the main power packs on all three were dead. Design fault. Of course it shouldn't happen, and of course among all the million bits of design and engineering it does. It nearly finished us. We charged up the auxiliary pack on this one as high as we could and rode it into the station, watching the power gauge dropping all the time. It had reached twelve per cent by the time we docked. I had been praying aloud from thirty per cent downwards.'

'You could have left it and walked.'

There was a slight pause before she answered.

'We could have done. In the last resort we'd have had to try. Average surface temperature's thirty-eight K. That ground's trying to suck your heat right out through your boots. In theory these suits are capable at those temperatures. But you can't stop all conduction. And it's ice. Treacherous. You slip, you break something, you lie there, in the end you die if we don't reach you. And what are the rest of us going to do – carry you? Over the ice? We don't walk outside the station. At all. If any of us have to go out, we go in this crawler, fully pressurized, with a utility leading the way. And everyone else on standby.'

'I see.'

'No sightseeing trips here, Munro.'

'No.' He frowned. 'Earth should send another.'

'They will – eventually. Don't forget that if we need something that isn't on the resupply schedule, it's eight years' wait before it can get here. And when its launch slot comes up, it may get bumped off by something that's higher priority – a new telmex, for example.'

She uncoupled the charging cable. She faced him.

'Would the new telmex like a ride?'

The new telmex. It was a strange way to say 'you'. It was playful, in a way. He had not heard her sound like that before.

'Yes,' he said.

The hatch on the rear of the red crawler opened on a voice command. There was a tiny airlock. Beyond it the interior was a low chamber with two forward-facing seats at one end. Two bench-seats for passengers ran down either side. There were controls at the pilot seats but no windows. Instead, a screen showed visual displays of the exterior when powered by command.

'Hello, living quarters?' said Vandamme. 'We're taking the red crawler.'

'I've got you,' said Lewis's voice, as clearly as if they had all been sitting together back in the common room. 'Have fun.'

'Do we pressurize the cabin?' asked Paul.

'Yes,' Vandamme replied. 'Normally we wouldn't, just to ride around inside the station. But you need to know how it works in case you're ever part of an outside mission. The important thing is, even if the cabin is pressurized you do *not* remove your helmet or depressurize your suit. That's for safety. Of course the cabin shouldn't depressurize, but conditions here are extreme and accidents are always possible. So – to pressurize, it's this sequence . . .'

At first nothing seemed to happen. And then the numbers on the helmet display flickered. He watched them. The one marked *Suit* remained at 1.0. But the one marked *Ex* – the exterior pressure – rose rapidly. Now it was over 0.8 and still rising. The temperature was rising too.

'That's the auxiliary battery gauge,' said Vandamme. 'You can see we're already bleeding it down.'

A bright green bar showed on the crawler display. Over it there were the figures *97%*. Even as Paul watched it dropped to *96%*. He looked away.

'Short trips only, you see,' said Vandamme. 'Now, to go forward . . .' She demonstrated. The crawler hummed into life. The display inside Paul's helmet read *Ex: 1.0 Suit: 1.0 Temp: -10°*. There was an atmosphere around him, cold and crisp, but enough to let sound travel inside the cabin. The crawler was creeping forward with astonishingly little inertia for so massive a thing. The screen showed the far end of the hangar approaching.

'Beyond that seal you're into the outer layers,' said Vandamme. 'There's nothing out there – they're just for protection and maintaining the insulation–conduction balance. If you like we could step out there on the way back. It's quite a thrill the first time you see your helmet display drop into Kelvin. It can get all the way down to ninety at times.'

'Ninety! Is it liquid out there?'

The transmission was so clear that he actually heard her grin.

'Oxygen at normal atmospheric pressure will liquefy at about ninety K,' she said. 'But it's not that simple. Our doctor once took a tube of air from the living quarters out there because she wanted to see what happened to it. What she forgot was that the pressure in those chambers is never more than point four, so all that happened was that the tube shattered, the gas escaped and she was showered with shards. She was lucky her suit wasn't damaged. And our station manager was furious.'

Our doctor. Our station manager. Again she was using functions instead of names. This time the emphasis had been different. It might have been mockery.

There had been hints of this before – of friction

between the three of them. *Was it my fault she lost Thorsten?*

Friction? Deep, bitter resentment, barely suppressed. Did they blame her for Thorsten's death? He remembered how they had leaped to answer his questions about Thorsten in that first meeting, as if protecting Vandamme from a suggestion he had not intended to make. What kind of a partner let her man despair? Perhaps May felt guilt that Lewis was living when Thorsten was dead. Yes! She must hate that, and she was blaming Vandamme for the blame she felt on herself. And so on, round and round, a destructive feedback loop in the heart of the station. It had been going on for years with no escape.

And then the spacecraft from Earth had brought them another man, mumbling, confused, barely able to say more than 'Yes' and 'No'. It had been the biggest birthday present ever, May had said. And Vandamme had walked away from it. She had shut herself in the other chambers, which must be heated and pressurized for her at whatever cost to the station's energy supply. And she prayed. And she worked. And she filled the walls with images of desolation.

His eyes flicked to the woman beside him, and away again before she could realize he was looking at her. A trickle of sympathy oozed from the icy crust around his heart.

Did she know what the others were planning for her? Had she realized what they were trying to do?

What would she think, if he told her?

The display swung as the crawler turned. Now it faced across the hangar, to a seal in the side wall. The crawler flowed smoothly towards it.

'You can open the seals by voice, or by signal,' said Vandamme. 'That key there. You do it.'

Paul pressed the key in the panel. The seal opened, revealing one of the small airtight chambers that linked each bubble in the station to its neighbours. Paul peered at it. It was hard to judge the size of it through the screen.

'Will we fit in this?' he asked.

'We will – just.'

She inched the machine forward, checked the rear display and closed the door they had just passed through. The door ahead opened automatically.

Paul let out a long sigh.

'So – here's our farmland,' said Vandamme. 'What do you think?'

It was like a huge, old-fashioned polytunnel, of the kind that was still used in some places on Earth to cultivate crops when the exterior temperature was too low. Paul had visited one once. He still remembered the shock of smell when he had stepped through the flaps and stood in the forest of green plants, bursting with green and reddening tomatoes, and stretching away before him under the roof of arched plastic. It had been strong enough to break through and impose itself over all the busy messaging of his World Ear. That rich, warm scent – he could almost smell it now. It had stamped itself into his memory for ever.

But this tunnel had no leaves and no fruits. The light was a dull grey-blue, filtering through the translucent layers above his head. The floor of the bubble was littered with low lumps of rubble that must have been left over from the construction process. Pathways as straight as furrows carved through them. On one, halfway along the tunnel, a harvester was working. It looked like a grey, man-made insect, intent on something among the stones. Vandamme coasted the red crawler forward and switched the screen to give a side-view so that Paul could see the thing clearly.

It had stopped by a lump that seemed to Paul to be like any other lump on the floor of that tunnel. One grey arm had extended. It was moving slowly across the face of the lump, just as if it were giving the thing a shave. Paul could see how the colour of the surface had changed where the arm had already been.

'A basic lichen, modified to grow under these conditions,' said Vandamme. 'It provides thirty to forty per cent of our foodstuffs. A side-product of the process produces our fabrics when we need them. It also contributes to the ecological balance of the station. But it's mainly for

136

nutrition. That might be tomorrow's breakfast, being picked for you now.'

'Do we grow nothing more . . . ?' Paul fumbled for a suitable word.

'Advanced? Eatable? Complicated?'

'More normal.'

'You mean, the sort of things we would normally have eaten on Earth? No. It's a question of economy. To do that you would have to heat and pressurize these bubbles to the same level as the living quarters. That would be an enormous energy demand. On top of that there would still have to be further bubbles outside them, to insulate them and also to bring down that pressure gradually so that if there's an impact we don't get a catastrophic rupture. Oh, and you would have to have a depth of soil, full of vegetable matter and nutrients – all that.'

On the screen, the harvester withdrew its arm and rolled away a few metres down the path. It stopped by another lump.

'There are a number of high-pressure bubbles just above the living quarters,' said Vandamme. 'Some of them we've turned over to cultivating stimulants and flavourings – the stuff that goes into our coffee, for example. It doesn't make real coffee, of course. It's a substitute. But it's not bad if you don't drink too much of it.'

'How long will the machines function?'

'With regular maintenance they should have an operating life of approximately fifteen years. But remember that three hundred per cent redundancy. If one breaks down early, we just replace it while Lewis works out what went wrong.'

Fifteen years, and another forty-five years from the reserve machines made sixty. The station had already lasted ten years, so it had another fifty years before anyone left in it starved, or came out to pick lichens by hand. What else would last fifty years in this place? The power plant? The waste recycling? The door seals? Some chambers had failed and were disused. The station was already trading on its redundancy. But then no one knew how long a human body would last here either.

It was madness, what they were doing. She must see that. She would have more reason to see it than Lewis or May.

'So – would you like to drive it back?' said Vandamme.

'. . . All right.'

'You don't have to turn it. Just put it into reverse. I'll change the view . . . there.'

The joystick in the control panel was enormous – two to three times the size of the control on his monitor. He took it in his clumsy great gauntlet and it worked easily.

'That's reverse,' said Vandamme. 'Now, at your feet there are two pedals. Press firmly but don't stamp . . . That's right.'

Paul had a sensation of moving backwards. Confusingly, the end of the chamber on his screen was coming closer.

'This is *fun*!' said Vandamme, with a cheerfulness that was almost eerie, springing so suddenly from her lips. 'Bye-bye, breakfast. See you tomorrow. And let us thank God for his goodness. "I'll not want, for he makes me lie down in green pastures, he leads me beside quiet waters . . ."'

'There are no waters,' said Paul.

'There are,' she said, and he could tell she was grinning. 'Once we've returned the crawler I'll show you.'

The ceiling of this bubble was a blaze of light, like a roof of opaque glass on a sunny day. The glare was filtering down through at least three layers of transparent bubble-wall, so all definition was lost and it was impossible to pick out the structure of the sun mirror, poised on the roof of the station far above their heads. Even to look up was to wince. Paul tried to shade his eyes with his hand. His gauntlet bumped clumsily against the visor of his helmet and did no good.

The floor of the bubble was a tank like a long, thin swimming pool, surrounded by a walkway with a handrail. The water was a murky brown. The air was full of steam. His vision blurred as a layer of droplets formed on his helmet. Under the mirror the air was as warm as a mild Earth day. And the pressure was near normal. If it was any less, the rate of evaporation would increase and precious water would be lost to the station.

'What's in the tank?' he asked.

'Algae, again. The simplest, single-celled varieties. The base of any food chain.'

'This goes into the lichen-feed?'

'Primarily this. Also expired or defective lichen harvests, and of course our own waste – anything organic.'

So we are eating our own shit, thought Paul. At just one remove. It should neither have surprised nor revolted him but it did. And the 'coffee' that they drank – which was not coffee but a substitute, a lie like all the other lies in the station – that had shit in it too.

'We're right over the living quarters now,' Vandamme said. 'Obviously this arrangement helps keep the living quarters warm. It also means we can have conventional water-based sanitary systems rather than anything working on vacuum. It wasn't done for our comfort but it's nice when something works out in our favour for once.'

'Can I take off my helmet?' he said.

She hesitated. But in almost eighty per cent of an atmosphere there would be no risk. It would be like standing on the top of a mountain on Earth.

'You want to sniff the air? I warn you, it's pretty fetid. All right. Living quarters? We're up in the tanks. Munro is going to remove his helmet. I think it's safe.'

'Very good,' came Lewis's voice.

'So,' she said. 'You check the external pressure. Never mind if you've done it already, you do it again. Now you unlock the suit controls and take the suit pressure down to the exterior pressure – slowly, or you'll do yourself damage . . .'

Paul made a sequence of touches on the suit control at his chest. There was a faint hissing noise from somewhere. His ears rang, and then shrieked with pain and popped. His display read: *Ex: 0.8 Suit: 0.8.*

'Done that? Now you power down the suit—'

He touched the control again. Vandamme's voice was cut off. His display disappeared and the weight of the suit on his limbs and shoulders suddenly increased. His fingers found the lock on his helmet. He twisted, lifted the helmet free – and gasped.

The air *was* fetid. It stank. The brown soup in the tank gave off a sour, musty smell, which rose with the steam from the surface and was hauled all the way down his throat as his lungs heaved at the thin air.

He looked down at his hands and saw that his gauntlets – his whole suit in fact – was covered with tiny water droplets, which had condensed out of the atmosphere.

When he looked closer he saw that the droplets were ice. The exterior of his suit had been exposed to temperatures well below freezing for over an hour. So had Vandamme's. She stood beside him like a statue made of ice, with a grotesque, blind, outsized head. Her face was lost inside the veil of her visor. She glistened in the overhead glare. When she moved, her limbs shimmered with light.

He put his hand to her visor and clumsily wiped away the crystals. Dimly now, he could see her eyes and nose within. He signed for her to take her helmet off.

For a moment she did not respond. So he tapped on her visor and signed again.

She shook her head. There must be some safety procedure: at least one member of the party must be suited and pressurized at all times – something like that. Paul didn't care. He had decided to take the risk of talking to her. So she should take a risk to listen.

He tapped and signed again, more urgently. *Take it off*, he mouthed.

She stood there in front of him. Inside her helmet, her lips were moving. She must be consulting Lewis. Paul did not want her to consult Lewis. The whole point was that if she took her helmet off, no one in the living quarters would hear what he had to say.

Take it off! he screamed silently into her face.

Her hands moved. They touched the buttons on her controls. He saw the little jets of air, warm from inside her suit, melting long streaks of droplets down her legs as she reduced the pressure. Then her hands lifted and the helmet came off, revealing the upper half of her face peering out from inside the high, circular suit-collar.

'Munro? What is the matter?'

'I want to talk to you.'

She frowned. 'What about?'

'About May. And Lewis. They want to have a child.'

'Oh God – that! Why do I have to talk about that?'

'You knew?'

'Yes I did,' she said shortly. 'Did they tell you?'

'I guessed.'

'You haven't guessed all of it then. She's pregnant.'

Pregnant.

'About nine weeks, she thinks. Is this what you wanted to say? I thought it was something urgent – something you wanted me to see or smell.'

'It is urgent! If she's pregnant it is *more* urgent!'

'Can't we do this in the living quarters?'

'Not so easily.'

'I see.'

She was angry – angry about May, and angry with him for wanting to talk about it.

143

'All right,' she said. 'What do you want to say?'

'She will die! In this gravity it's . . . it's stupid. There's no one to help!'

'Do you think she doesn't know there's a risk? She's our doctor, after all. Who knows better than she?'

'She wants it too much to see the risk!'

'Are you a medic, Munro?'

'No.'

No, but he was learning to think for himself. He was learning not to rely on networks and data, because there were none. Nor would he rely on experts. May might be a doctor but she was not dispassionate. The baby was one of the 'wonderful things' she believed in. It must be the biggest of them all. Therefore she could not be suspicious of it.

Childbirth put the bodies of mother and baby under enormous stress. It was the fault of the human brain. It had to grow to a size larger than could be contained inside the mother. The baby had to be protected as long as possible, so it was kept inside the mother until the last moment and then forced out through the narrow channel of the pelvic bones. So tight was the fit of the baby's head that its skull was squeezed out of shape during its passage.

In one-tenth of Earth's gravity, with bones attenuated to a fraction of their strength – what would happen to mother and child then?

'It *is* possible, Munro. There was a successful birth on Mars station. That's what made them finally decide to try it.'

He had not known that. It must have happened during his long sleep. But it did not make any difference.

'Van – Mars has more than *four times* our gravity! They have hundreds of people. Medical teams, operating theatres . . . It's madness here! Worse, it's our doctor! Who can help her when it goes wrong?'

'All right! Look, I'll agree it's dangerous! But it's no use us saying that. It's her choice. It's what she's always wanted. Do you think you could persuade her not to go ahead? Anyway, it's already happening. It would be a risk even for her to stop at this stage. Abortion is not straightforward, even if she was prepared to do it. And she isn't.'

'She doesn't know the science,' said Paul roughly. 'She's a medic, but this is not her field. If she understood the risks—'

'For God's sake! I don't want to talk about this – can't you see? I can't talk to them about it and they wouldn't listen if I did! All I can do for them is pray. And I *am* praying, believe me!'

'Earth would know the risks,' he persisted. 'If Earth—'

'Munro!'

She had checked in the act of replacing her helmet. Now she was looking at him as if he had hit her.

'You must not tell Earth. You must not.'

'Why not?'

'Because Earth is evil,' she said flatly.

They stood face to face by the pool where life was beginning.

'You must not tell Earth,' she repeated.

His message had gone out over the laser the previous day. He did not tell her. She would find out soon enough.

They all would.

XI

They sat opposite him in a row in the main bubble of the living quarters, all three of them.

Lewis, tight-lipped, was in the middle. In his hand he held a printout. Printouts were rare in the station, where all consumables were derived from the same supply of lichens and all manufacturing processes drew on the same precious sources of energy. The crew did not use printouts unless they thought it was important. Lewis's eyes flicked repeatedly down to it and up to Paul again. Only the redness of his cheeks and the soft clip of his voice as he arranged the crew in their places gave any hint of his fury.

May's cheeks were flushed too. There was a bright-red spot in the centre of each of them and the rest of her face was pale. She did not look at Paul at all. She looked at her feet. Her hair was tied back so that her ears showed. Her hands were in her lap. Paul looked at her belly and wondered if the slight swelling there was the first visible sign of the baby, or if it had always been like that. He could not remember.

He told himself that they could do nothing to him. They could do nothing that they had not already done when he had been picked out of the living air of Earth and sent to this place.

'All right, let's start,' said Lewis.

He handed the printout to Vandamme.

'This came in on my last watch,' he said. 'I could not immediately see which aspect of the station's function it was referring to, so I interrogated the message-bank. It turned out to be a reply to two messages Paul had sent over the laser.

'Paul, do you recall the message you sent to Earth at twenty-eight: zero three: sixteen zero three?'

'Yes.'

'And the one at twenty-nine: zero three: eleven thirty-two?'

'Yes.'

'Perhaps you would say what the contents were.'

Nerves were constricting Paul's throat. He fought the impulse to clear it.

'I told Earth that I thought you and May were planning a child, and that you had lied to Earth about the chances for more generations here. In the second message I said she was pregnant. I asked for instructions.'

He made himself look at Vandamme then. The first message had gone before they had taken off their helmets by

148

the algae-bath. The second had gone later, after she had told him that it mattered more than anything that Earth should not know.

She nodded once. Her expression was blank.

'I am tempted to ask what instructions you thought Earth might give,' said Lewis.

Paul looked at the printout in Vandamme's hand. The message seemed to be quite short. He had expected something much longer, containing medical analyses, predictions, images, graphs, statistics, all pointing firmly towards an inescapable conclusion. He was itching to know what it did say. But to ask would be weakness.

'The best course for us,' he said.

'Again I am tempted to ask who you mean by *us*.'

Paul clamped his jaw shut. He was not going to play this game.

'It must have been clear to you, Paul, that we wanted her pregnancy to be kept confidential, and above all that we did not want it revealed to Earth. It should also have been clear to you that the four of us depend absolutely on each other's cooperation. If you suspected that we were embarked on a course that you thought unwise, it should have been your duty to consult with us first and find out our reasons. Instead, you informed Earth at the earliest possible opportunity. Why?'

'You had lied to Earth.'

'I have good reasons for what I've done. If you ask me I'll tell you. But I want to know what yours are.'

Paul looked at the printout again. What did it *say?*

'Because of the risk,' he told them.

'What can Earth do about the risk? It takes eight years for a ship to reach us! We are completely beyond any help that Earth might send. You know that perfectly well. What did you think Earth would say?'

Vandamme returned the printout to Lewis, who passed it on to May. May read it, and Paul watched her as she did so. She did not look up at him. She put it carefully down on the table. She rose. Still she did not look at him. With long, slow skips she left the room.

In the silence Paul reached across and drew the printout across to him. It read:

01:04:1337 Your 28:03:1603 and 29:03:1132. Congratulations. Relevant updates will be transmitted to your files. Keep us informed. Good luck. Ends.

'I suppose you thought they would order an abortion,' said Lewis coldly. 'You must have known we would not wish it, but you thought you could get Earth to overrule us. You wanted it to bombard us with World-Ear knowledge, so that in the end we would be persuaded despite ourselves. But it wouldn't have worked. I've thought about this for years. Nothing Earth could say would persuade me now.

'And you don't understand Earth, Paul. It is not interested in us as people. It thinks of us as a thing. A seed. As long as it thought the seed was sterile, it would have left us alone. Now it knows we have begun to germinate. It will watch us more closely. It will think about expanding the colony and about how to get the World Ear to function out here after all. This is the worst possible thing you could have done.'

'She will die,' said Paul harshly.

'I *know* there's a risk! Do you think I don't care? Do you think she doesn't know it? She is a very, very brave woman! But we both know this is the only future there is.'

'Future? What future?'

'For humanity. We are the last humans left. Don't you see that? We are the last chance to build a community in which individuals are free to respect one another. And we can! We have the mistakes of Earth for our guide. We can observe the norms and behaviours that inoculate us against the disease of the We. But that's no good if it stops with the four of us! If it stops with us, we've failed! Don't you *see* how much it matters?'

'You are crazy,' Paul said. 'Mad.'

'Think about what you're saying, Paul. Just think

about it. If we die out, that's the *end*. There's no one else.'

'Mad! This won't work!'

'Mad? What do you mean by mad? Which of us is *mad*, Paul? An ant will go mad if it is taken from its nest. But a human taken from his community will build himself another one, however he can. Are you ant or human, Paul?'

'You want to breed more people,' said Paul, reddening. 'You have to make a bigger station. You can't do that.'

'What do *you* know about how many people the station can hold? Which chambers I can pressurize, heat and keep in balance? With three hundred per cent redundancy I could support another twelve people without even trying! They could be there now and you wouldn't know the difference!'

'So you jam the radio to make Earth send you a telmex! What next? Will you breed a new virus, to make them send us a microbiologist? Break the computers to make them send an engineer? Man, woman, man, woman – yes?'

Lewis stared at him. 'What are you saying, Paul? What the hell are you saying?'

'You said Earth sends people into space to make children. No. That was a lie. It was not Earth's idea. It was yours. *You got me sent here to help you breed!*'

'Paul – I had nothing to do with that!'

'Then why do you jam the transmissions?'

'I do not jam the transmissions. That's the field!'

'It is not the field! It is you!'

'By God, you *are* mad! Why would I waste my time doing that?'

'Lewis,' said Paul furiously. 'This child of yours—'

'You mean the one *you* wanted to kill?'

'This child – *if* it lives – will you tell it, all the time it grows, that there is hope? Will you tell it that it can run the machines, seal in the air, eat the lichens and go on living to have children of its own? And when you are gone, what will it think of you, as the systems fail one after another? When the bubbles are empty and everyone is gone, and it is the last thing there is? What do you think it will do? Go out into the outer chambers and take off its helmet like Thorsten? And as the air escapes, will it say, *I'm sorry, Daddy, I've failed?*'

'God! Right, that's enough! You have *no* idea, Paul! You just have *no* idea . . . It's no use talking to you.'

Lewis got up and stalked out of the common room.

Paul clenched and unclenched his fists. He was trembling with rage. He was trembling at the things he himself had said. Death. Long, lingering failure. Madness . . . The crew moved in this pocket of air and never spoke about those things. They talked about coffee and magnetism, radio signals and God. They told each other that they must be like family and then they shrieked at each other and ran off to hide in their rooms. They never spoke about how close they lived to Death. Now he had called it into the room. Lewis had made him do it. Earth and Lewis between them.

He looked at the printout again.

Congratulations. Relevant updates will be transmitted to your files. Keep us informed.

He heard himself say, 'What updates?'

'It will be medical data,' said Vandamme quietly. 'Lessons learned from the case on Mars. Studies. How to cheat our own biology, and achieve a live birth despite the odds.'

Paul was still staring at the printout. The cold, un-surprised banality of it touched him like an icy finger. *Oh, you* are *having a child then, are you? Someone's risking their life for it, are they? Very good.*

Carry on and let us know how it goes.

'So Earth wants this child too.'

'For its own purposes, yes.'

Once again he had been betrayed. This time it was Earth who had betrayed him.

'It's a dilemma,' she mused. 'Earth is a terrible thing. Evil. We should not deal with it at all. But we are not fully self-sufficient here. There has to be some resupply. So we cannot help it – we have to depend upon the beast. If the beast can help save a life here on the station, should we not ask for help? What will the price for that help be? They fear the answer. So do I. This is why they were angry with you. But if you had not done it, maybe in three months' time they would have done it themselves.'

Congratulations, whispered the printout.

'And our observations here,' she went on. 'What about them? If God gave me a gift, it was my science. But what I do here is meaningless if I keep it to myself. I *must* send it to Earth. There is nowhere else for it to go. So I too am feeding the beast. I am making it stronger, even though it is the enemy of all of us. And if you press me on this, I may lose my temper just like he did. Because I too do not know the answer. And I'm afraid of what it might be.'

Keep us informed.

'What will you do now?' she asked him.

He opened his fingers and let the printout float gently away. 'Why do you ask?'

'I think you will do something wrong. I wonder if I can persuade you not to.'

'Wrong?'

'To them.'

'I thought you did not like them.'

She frowned at that, as if he had suggested some puzzle that was difficult but that ought to be soluble.

'Some of the time I hate them,' she said. 'You've seen that.

155

It isn't just because I love science and I love prayer that I keep myself to myself here. Why do I hate them? I think it's because they're what God wanted. There – I've confessed it now! Maybe He will forgive me at last. They're as He meant us to be – even though they don't know Him. I am not. You are not. My God – did they really want us to be partners?'

They looked at each other, in the quiet of the central chamber.

'We're opposites,' she said. 'You have come from the We. I am alone.' She put her hand to her head. 'I am a little mad, maybe. I sometimes think I am.'

Paul nearly said: *It is mad to believe in God.* But he did not, because she was the last connection he had left. Instead he said, 'It is mad to think a new generation could survive here.'

Again she frowned. 'How do you know?'

'It is obvious.'

'Have you looked at that assessment he sent to Earth?'

'No.'

'He was very clever when he wrote that. Everything he said was true. Yet he said the opposite of what he believed. Yes, the challenge is immense. If they want to do it without Earth's help it is worse still. How can they? We're far, far too few. We can't make new machines, or new fuel or new seals. It would mean cannibalization of machinery, adaptation, rationing: years of gradual descent into a caveman-like existence . . .

'But it suits him, you see,' she added sourly. 'It gives him everything he wants. He's got his partner. He has a noble cause. And he has command. He *calls* it "cooperation", but that's only his style. In ten years not one of us ever stood up to him in the way you did just now. How can he not be heroic? It's the sort of thing men dream of, isn't it?'

'I dream of Earth,' said Paul. 'And my child.'

'But Earth is lost!' she said. 'The generations born there are lost before they can even open their eyes!'

She sighed.

'And yet . . . Look at this place! He's going to conscript his child into carrying it on. Can you imagine a child here? Poor thing – peering out at all that ice! And after we've all gone, like you said, what will happen? You could hate them for what they're doing.'

'There doesn't have to be one here,' said Paul carefully.

She looked at him.

'There doesn't have to be. If you help me. There will be a way.'

She was still looking at him. Her lips moved. He thought she was tempted. He thought that she would ask, *What way?* And he would say that he did not know yet. But there would be one if the two of them were able to think of it together.

She did not speak. Her eyes went to the table top. She put her hands out on it and looked at the backs of them together. She drew breath.

'Oh God!' she said. 'And for a moment I was sorry for you! But the two of you – thumping your chests at each other like ape-men from a million years ago! And now you want to stifle his children! That's how our race started. Is it how we're going to finish?'

'No!' He jumped up. 'I'm trying to save her *life*!'

'You think so? Maybe you're not like him then. At least he's honest with himself. Maybe you're like me after all. And that *does* make me sorry for you! But God sees into my heart. And He sees into yours! He sees that you want to *punish* them for being what you're not! *Can't you hear what you've said?*'

They were both on their feet, eye to eye. In the silence the low hum of the station systems crept back into the air of the common room.

'You are angry,' said Paul, 'because you want to agree with me.'

She stared at him. Then she turned away. She took two long paces down the chamber. She looked back at him.

'I know who you are now,' she said.

'I thought you were just a poor man. You'd had so much robbed from you, when they planted the World Ear and when they took it away again, that you were still finding out what it is to be human – what's right and what's wrong. But you're not. You're very, very clever. You're the cleverest of all God's creatures. And the worst.'

Her words sank inside him, turning and turning like objects falling into deep water, bumping into nothing. Nothing would stop their descent until they rested on the muddy floor of his soul.

'Why have you followed me here?' she said.

'I don't know what you mean.'

'I should pray for you,' she said. 'I should try. But I don't think I can.'

XII

He had tried to kill the child.

The thought stopped him in the middle of a coding sequence. He looked at the walls of his chamber. His fingers hovered but did not touch his keys.

The wall-display showed the hard blue sky and the pale grasses of the Hunter's savannah. He had chosen it after returning here from the crew meeting. He had chosen it because he too was hunting.

He was recoding the lost groups from the last set of tail data for transmission by laser. He had not found any suitable translation program in the station's resources and he had not sent for one from Earth because he did not want to risk alerting the others to what he was doing. Therefore he had to recode the radio signals for the laser by hand – keystroke after keystroke, *tap, tap, tap*, pausing every now and then to check for the errors that seemed to creep in, however careful he was.

It was tedious. It was mind-numbing. Even after his mind

had learned the routines and had passed the task on to those areas of the brain that would run them automatically, it was taking more than an hour to code a second's worth of transmission. But time was one of the few resources he had. And as he worked, his thoughts drifted, like an unpiloted vessel through space, until they struck something.

He had tried to kill the child.

He had a child of his own, on Earth.

The grasses waved silently. In the mid-distance the squat, misshapen trees shimmered in the imagined heat. He could not feel it. His senses were like his conscience. They noted that things existed but they could not persuade him that they were real.

No! He had not *wanted* to kill the child. What he had *wanted* was that May should not have the child. That their plan should be upset. That their lie should be exposed. He had assumed that the child would die anyway. Why? May was ready to risk her life. Everyone else would let her do so. Even Earth had offered its distant congratulations as she steered for her passage with death.

He had barely left his room since the meeting. He had not eaten at all that evening, or this morning either. He was lonely and bewildered, and consumed with a fear that he knew nothing at all. This sense of *not knowing* was terrible. He did not know who was interfering with the signals, or why. He did not know if May would live, or if her child would live, or how long any of them would live out here.

A hunter must be alone. To want anything else was weakness.

He had opened the microphone channel to the common room, on low volume, so that he would be warned of anyone approaching his door. So when May spoke out there, suddenly and in distress, he heard her.

'Why did he say that?' she cried. 'Why?'

A lower voice answered her. To his surprise Paul realized that it was not Lewis but Vandamme.

'It's not true!' May exclaimed.

Again the murmur of Vandamme's voice.

'But it doesn't have to be!' May was almost in tears. '*You* could do something about that! You could!'

Curious, Paul opened the video link to the common room and increased the volume. He was in time to see May disappearing through her chamber door. Lewis was standing in the common room with his hands on his hips. The top of Vandamme's head was in the very corner of Paul's screen.

'That was unkind, Van,' Lewis said.

Vandamme's head disappeared. She must have turned away from him.

'Van!' Lewis called.

The only answer was the hiss of the airlock seal.

'Hunter,' said Paul.

The grasses parted. The Hunter stood in the working area before him.

'Find me the word *evil,* used about the World Ear.'

Hunter looked at him for a second. Then the ape-like mouth moved. Vandamme's voice spoke in the room. '*I have finally understood the full evil of the We . . .*'

'That's it. Show me.'

It was an entry that she had added to the Knowledge Store.

WS2: 20:03:1118 I have finally understood the full evil of the We. It means that the whole human race has lost its Free Will. Free Will is not just the ability to make a choice. Without Free Will no relationship with God is possible. All He has taught us has been lost and His sacrifice for us has proved to be in vain. The We is the last triumph of Satan.

'It's not about child killing,' Paul murmured.

'*Do you wish me to search—*'

'No.'

Paul studied Vandamme's entry. It had been written the day she had met him. It had been in him that she had finally seen the evil that the We had done.

But he did not understand what she meant. On Earth he

had been making choices all the time. That was how it had seemed to him. It was just that on Earth, equipped with the World Ear, the choices had been far, far easier than they were here. All he had needed to do was consult until the answers became obvious.

Linked to Vandamme's entry was a short exchange between her and Lewis.

WS1: 20:03:1334 So we should re-name our station 'Eden'? Is that what you are saying, Van?

WS2: 20:03:1357 Eden at thirty degrees Kelvin? 'Ark' might be better. And I shall set my display to a rainbow to remind me of God's promise.

WS1: 20:03:1540 I don't recall that story in detail. But you prompt me to wonder whether the We itself might contract some kind of spiritual life – or at least start looking for a purpose. There's a suggestion in the last download that it can imagine bringing about the next Big Bang. If so, it would have secured – at least in its own mind – its place as an indispensable aspect of the universe. The universe created it so that it can create the next universe. That's purpose for you.

WS2: 20:03:1712 You don't 'contract' a spiritual life. You 'contract' diseases.

WS1: 20:03:1726 My point entirely, Van. Although in the case of the We, it might be more of a genetic disorder.

Vandamme appeared to have broken off the contact at that point. Her next entry sequentially read:

WS2: 20:03:2100 Borehole achieved by Search Crawler 14 at 51.975' N, 34.695' W. No content.

And the next was from May:

WS3: 20:03: 2234
Alpha, beta, gamma
Particle and ray,
The Sun has boiled the sea,
The sky is stripped away.
Naked in the dust.
Infinity returns.
And I will cradle you, my love,
My love, my little love,
While all creation burns.

My love, my little love. That meant her child. Hers and Lewis's. The one they said he had wanted to kill.

He hadn't meant . . .

Useless to protest. They would decide what he had meant. For them, only that would be the truth.

Paul gritted his teeth. He went to Vandamme's entries about her god and searched them for the word 'evil'. There were so many occurrences that he did not look at any of them. Instead he searched for the words she had said in the crawler, about *quiet waters*. He found them. He found other words around them, about paths and green pastures – and the shadow of death. He supposed they were what Vandamme had meant by 'prayer'.

After a little, he went back to the string of Vandamme/ Lewis entries. He began to construct an entry of his own.

A date-time group sprang up automatically. *WS4: 03:04:1134.*

He looked at it for a moment, then shrugged and dragged the keyboard towards him. Frowning with concentration, he started to spell out what he wanted to say. *About Lewis's 20:03:1540. The plan on Earth is to . . .*

The words were not right. They did not capture how things worked in the scientific communities. The word 'plan' was too certain. He tried again.

Some scientists have proposed . . .

That was wrong too. That put the emphasis on individuals. It did not recognize the thousands of reactions that each proposal would have received, or the part they would have played. Feedback was at least half of anything that happened in the World Ear.

Words were the problem. There were World Ear symbols for the thing he wanted to express but he could think of no exact translation. And then there was the keyboard – the damned, wretched, primitive keyboard! It slowed him down. It made his silent speech the more halting. He felt he had receded almost to the state in which he had first arrived at the station, capable of saying 'Yes' and 'No' and little else.

But it was better than coding. Anything was better than coding.

The idea is . . . he tapped.

That was as close as he could come to it in a few words. The Idea. A series of proposals, met by a storm of feedback from peer communities. An idea was something that *might* be – that could not be achieved yet, but that was retained in the consciousness as a possible future action, for when circumstances were right.

The idea is that we . . .

He hesitated over 'we'. But he did not want to use 'it', or 'the We', as the others would have done.

The idea is that we achieve the first Big Bang. We will be the creators of our own universe.

'Paul?'

He jumped. It was Lewis.

It was Lewis, speaking over the intercom, but his voice had sounded so present that Paul had automatically blanked his screen.

'Yes?'

Lewis's voice filtered coldly into the room.

'I'm shuffling the watches. Will you stand in for Van at the next passage of the tail?'

Paul thought.

'Yes.'

'Thank you. And something else. Are you listening?'

'Yes.'

'The interference was happening before Thorsten died. Yes?'

'Yes.'

'So how could it have been a plot to get you here – when we still had our telmex?'

Paul did not answer.

'It doesn't work, Paul,' said Lewis. 'Think about it.'

After that there was silence, so Paul decided he had gone. He flicked the screen back to the log entry he had written. He had been about to add more, but the interruption had broken his train of thought. Instead he called up transmission records of the station's first year, before Thorsten had died. He found reports of the interference. He found requests from his predecessor to Earth for a translation program to circumvent the problem. None had been sent, it seemed. That was strange.

But it might not be as it seemed. As station manager, Lewis had permissions to enter or amend any part of the system. The records Paul was looking at could have been planted for him to find. They could have been planted just moments before Lewis had called him.

Grimly, he began to code again.

Time passed. When he checked the external view, he saw that the shadow was creeping over the planet once more. The disc was narrowing to a downturned mouth. A great aurora glowed on the dark face, like a chain of nebulae in the blackness. Soon they would make the passage of the tail.

He stole out to collect a long-overdue meal and ate it in his room. He slept for a short while and woke to begin coding again. In his breaks he thought about evil, and about going insane.

He called up the station archive and looked for the biographies of the crew members: their photographs, their qualifications and their histories. He studied them carefully. None of them had any grounding in telemetry.

In Lewis's training record he found a minor degree in computer coding. Vandamme obviously had major degrees in dynamic meteorology, but prior to her assignment to the station only limited experience in radio astronomy. Her first name, the record reminded him, was *Erin*.

He noticed that May had been in her mid-twenties when the mission had been launched. Not counting the eight years of flight, when all body processes would have slowed, she would be thirty-five now. That was old for a first child, even on Earth, but not impossible. Lewis was older. Of all of them, Paul was the youngest. If he was the youngest, there might also come a time when he was the last.

He did not think so. He could imagine that future but he could not believe that it was real. The real future was the one in which the child lived and grew and became one of them. And that was a future he could not imagine, because he had no idea what the child would be like. Would he speak with it, perhaps even teach it things? How could he prepare it for its bleak life? Would it ever find out that he had argued against its birth? There was no knowing. It was pure potential, an unwritten record, a biography that did not exist.

He called up another entry. *91/926.2 639: Thorsten Bondevik.*

170

It was a long, solemn face, the shape of an upside-down tear drop, with a little mouth and chin and pronounced lines across the brow. The ears were small but they stuck out prominently from the side of the head. Like Lewis, Thorsten had been nearly bald. The photograph did not show him smiling. Looking at it, Paul wondered if his predecessor had ever smiled. He could not remember smiling himself – not since arriving here.

The entry said: *Deceased 11:03:1331 2057. Cause of death: asphyxiation following decompression of pressure suit.*

He wondered if he could ever come to the point when he would go to the outer layers and decompress his suit. He tried to imagine himself looking at the displays. *Ex: 0.3 Suit: 1.0 Temp: 90K*, and then he would bring his hand across to unlock his helmet. And the hiss of air and the sudden scream of pain in his ears as his tiny personal atmosphere exploded and was lost into the half-vacuum . . .

Even in his mind, his fingers refused to find the buttons. He looked into the eyes of the dead man and wondered what had happened that day in Thorsten's brain.

It was time for his watch.

He tapped in his entry codes immediately, so that Lewis would know he was on duty and would not be tempted to remind him. He tuned his monitor to the field readings. Then he adjusted the wall-display. The blue sky and yellow grasses vanished. All around him was darkness. In the dome over his head the tiny Sun was low over the crescent of the planet. He looked up at it.

There, somewhere there, a mere one hundred and fifty million kilometres from that point of light, was the place that should have been his home. It was so close to the Sun that it might have been one and the same: a tiny fleck of rock, a little gravity well just strong enough to cloak itself in a protective atmosphere, at exactly the right distance from its star for water to run freely on its surface and so for life to begin. And after four billion years, a form of life had evolved that was sufficiently intelligent to speak, to perceive the universe, and to step off the life-bearing rock and into the empty vastness around it. To send one of its number across space, to sit on another little rock, cold and empty, copying out strings and strings of numbers while a tiny seed of life stirred close by.

And now something else was happening back there. If he could view it not with his eye but with a radio telescope, he would see not one star but two. First with its primitive broadcasts and televisions, and latterly with its mobile networks and then the World Ear, the Earth had become a source of radio and microwave emissions almost as intense as the Sun itself. In the We, another new life had glowed into being. An infant yet, rising wobbly to its feet in the great dark room of space, looking around, beginning to wonder why it was alone.

It knew it must die. Some day, it too must come to an end. Why?

'I could feel sorry for you,' he murmured to the diamond spark. 'I could feel sorry. But you sent me here. You are my enemy, after all.'

There was a lump in his throat. He had been aware of it for some time. His body wanted to weep. He could feel his lips drawn back. His face muscles were bunched. His eyes were hot and runny. He hit the console with his fist – his weak, flimsy fist that sprang from his insect-thin arm. He was a victim, an object, an experiment. *What is it like, having the World Ear?* Vandamme had asked. And his answer: *You belong.*

He had been part of something much bigger. He had had purpose – something to which he could contribute. What purpose could an individual have by himself? A single *I*? Only to increase the *We*: the thing that was made of the millions of things called *I*. The *I* died for its tribe or nation. The parent lived and died for its child. The *I* must die. Only the *We* could live on.

And he had died, now. Once they had cut him off and put him in the rocket, his life within the We had ended. Death was the absence of life, just as dark was the absence of light and vacuum the absence of matter. What life could live out here, in this unanchored immensity, forty degrees above absolute zero? Death lay all around him. It lay in the bitter temperatures beyond the sealed doors of the station. It lay in the wastes of ice, uncloaked by atmosphere, naked to the emptiness of space. It held the frozen remains of a man up there in the blue-grey dusk on the canyon lip. The remains would not have decayed. Decay was only another form of life. Here, there was not even decay.

Now, in the darkness, he could believe what Lewis had said to him. Humanity was gone. For all those billions of human bodies, there was only one mind, callous, even oblivious of the individual cells that composed it. It had been there all the time. Perhaps it had been there even before the World Ear had let it leap to a new level of consciousness. It was a cold, stupid, animal brain. And it had dispensed with him. It had cast him out to where he could no longer belong. Why? Because it had been tricked by the crew? That did not work. For its own reproduction? That did not work either. There had been a man and two women here already. It must have had a reason and yet its reason was opaque. Its thoughts were slow. From the inside, in that swift and living stream of communications, he had never seen it. Only now, looking back from the very edge of the solar system, could he know that it was there.

They were deep into the tail. On his screen the impossible readings reeled away. He watched them with loathing.

The tail receded. The star hid itself beyond the canyon lip. The narrow crescent of the planet began to widen again, into a huge but ordinary half-moon. Paul completed coding the historical readings and sent them to the laser in the window that he would normally have used to transmit the passage data. At the same time he sent a dummy message over the radio, purporting to be the passage data but actually repeating readings that had been taken some days before on the Sun side. Then he slept, woke, slipped out of his room to pick up a meal from the kitchen and slipped back again before anyone saw him. He ate, waited, and then began to prepare the passage data for transmission. There was no hurry.

In a break he checked the Knowledge Store again. There were new entries.

WS1: 07:04:0556 Van, have you seen Paul's 03:04:1134?

WS2: 07:04:0617 I don't believe it! The We can't do that, can it? Reverse the arrow of time?

WS1: 07:04:0620 Why not? In time the We – or its successor – might be capable of anything.

WS2: 07:04:0622 But that would mean everything was just one huge paradox. Everything that has ever been just goes back on itself.

WS1: 07:04:0624 Strikingly egocentric, I agree. A symptom of loneliness, perhaps?

Again Vandamme had broken off the exchange.

Paul looked at the entries. He supposed they were contact of a sort. He saw that he could reply to them and let the others reply in turn. And at some point they might be able to talk to each other again – warily at first, perhaps, but then as if the argument had never happened.

It was what he had wanted. But now he could see that contact was possible, he did not want it. Not yet. First he must solve the interference with the transmissions. He must know who was doing it and why. When he knew, and they knew that he knew, he would speak with them again.

He waited.

At 08:04:0000 there was a watch-change. He checked the new schedules. Lewis and May were off. Vandamme was now on with him.

176

He waited a further hour and then sent the latest data from the tail out over the radio. He sent it with no preface, to minimize the possibility of anyone recognizing it for what it was.

Towards the end of his watch his monitor alerted him to an incoming message. It was a response to the signals he had sent out the previous day.

Your 07:04:1234 and 07:04:1238 received. No evident corruptions. But no apparent correlation. Query Observation DTGs. Also reference your 07:04:1234 query the following groups . . .

Earth was confused. It had received his two earlier messages clearly, including in the laser message the first unadulterated observations from the tail that the station had ever produced. But it did not understand what they related to, because he had not explained what he was doing. And it did not believe some of what it was reading.

Suddenly Paul grinned. It did not matter that Earth was confused. Earth was not the master here. He was. The nine-billion-celled brain was, for the moment, nothing more than his assistant. A servant, whose duty was to do just what it was told and whose questions did not matter. Is it corrupted, Earth, or is it not? You tell me it is not. Good. So I proceed . . .

It was a moment of sheer power, sweet in his mind.

Nevertheless he checked the groups Earth was querying and he did indeed find a few errors which had crept in despite his best attention. He signalled back his corrections, adding the dates and times at which the readings were taken so that Earth would at least know what it was he had sent, even if it did not yet know why. Then he went off watch.

He lay on his couch but did not sleep. Thoughts chased inside his head. It was good that the laser message had not been corrupted. He had smuggled out of the station information that was not meant to go to Earth. The theory that the laser was immune to interference was looking stronger. So he could simply send to Earth for a translation program, and tail data could be transmitted to Earth by laser for ever more.

But that was not what was important. If Earth had really wanted the tail data, the station would have had a translation program long ago. No program had been sent. To Earth, what was important was the corruption of the radio data. That was why Earth had sent him here – to have the best chance of finding out why it was happening. It was important to Paul too. The thought of a secret enemy was poison in his mind. Why had his radio message not been corrupted? Whatever the source of the interference, it was not triggered simply by the timing of the signal. Could it be capable of reading the message itself and seeing whether the content related to the tail? Would it detect the tail data that he had now sent out over the radio? Would it react to that? He needed it to react. Like a hunter crouched in the bush, he needed the beast to show itself.

The message was waiting for him when he woke.

> *Your 08:04:0102: Message corrupted. The following groups unreadable . . .*
> *. . . Investigate and report.*

'Got you!' he said.

XIII

The heavy figure of the ape-man filled his screen. In one hand the creature held its pointed stick – a pale wand of sharpened wood. It was so slender in the hairy hand that Paul wondered how it could possibly be lethal. And yet it would have been.

Behind the Hunter the grasses waved silently.

'Search all routines that were running at zero eight: zero four: zero one zero two,' said Paul. 'Report anything that might have corrupted radio transmission to Earth.'

The Hunter looked at him, unblinking.

'*There was nothing*,' it said.

'Nothing? You are sure?'

'*I have searched three million one thousand six hundred and eighty-two routines. All were benign.*'

'A radio message containing data on the tail was sent to Earth at zero eight: zero four: zero one zero two,' Paul insisted. 'It was corrupted, like all radio transmissions concerning the tail before it. Was this an accident, was it natural, or was it deliberate?'

'*It is highly likely that it was deliberate.*'

Paul let out his breath.

'I agree. But it was not done by an automatic routine?'

'*No.*'

'You are saying it was manual?'

'*It is highly likely.*'

Manual! So they – whoever it was – had done it by the oldest and most primitive way possible. They had watched or listened to what he was doing themselves. And then they had jammed his signal.

They were watching him. Whoever it was, they were watching him and acting when he acted. Incredible! And how primitive, how prone to error! But it was not vulnerable to detection by Hunter.

Or so they might think.

'We will replicate the transmission. Monitor all active workstations in the station and be ready to display what you find.'

He began to prepare a repeat of his signal. His fingers knew the commands and performed them automatically. His mind was alive with suspicions.

Lewis? He might know how to clean the transmitter records afterwards, so that no sign of the jamming signal remained. Or Vandamme? She would be able to identify tail data at a glance. She would have the patience, the machine-like focus to watch for the signal and act on it when it came – whenever it came.

Or was it May?

Was it all of them, all working together?

Shit!

Where was the signal coming from, anyway?

He got up and began to pace the room. He paced aimlessly. He muttered aloud. He went and fidgeted with his monitor. He left it again.

Shit!

He sat down. He checked the watch schedules. Vandamme and May were on. But if they were all in it, it didn't matter who was on. Hunter would have to watch for all of them.

'Show me all present workstation activity.'

'*There is a prohibition . . .*'

'Circumvent it.'

His screen changed immediately. It showed him a view of the hangar. A suited figure was bending over a partly dis-assembled crawler. That was what his human eyes saw. But it was not what Hunter would have seen. Hunter was relay-ing to him what another workstation was doing.

'Which workstation is that?'

'*Workstation Two*.' Vandamme's.

As if to confirm the thought, Vandamme's voice spoke. 'You're over your three hours. Do you want to come in?' And Lewis's voice answered, 'I'll get it finished. It shouldn't take much longer now.'

So Vandamme was supervising Lewis out in the hangar. Lewis was working past the three-hour advisory limit for his pressure suit, to finish the repair he was working on.

That only left May.

'Workstation Three?'

'*Inactive*.'

An inactive monitor might mean that May was asleep. But she should be on watch now. Where was she?

'It's showing some wear on the rear drive, there,' came Lewis's voice from the hangar. 'Maybe the wheel's out of kilter.'

Paul reverted to his own controls, called up the 08:04:0102 message and pressed *Dispatch*. Then he said, 'Hunter, display all workstation activity.' The screen flicked back to the hangar again.

'. . . the weak point in this design,' Lewis was saying. 'Irritating, when you think how much we depend on it.'

'Workstation Three, Hunter?' said Paul.

'*Inactive*.'

'What about Workstation One?' barked Paul. (Because

May could be in Lewis's room! Of course she could. He could be hiding there, watching Paul's signal at this moment . . .)

'*Workstation One is inactive.*'

'Good,' said Paul hoarsely. And he felt the prickle of sweat as his body reacted to the thought that he might have been outwitted. But he hadn't been. The monitors were inactive.

But he must think these thoughts. He must check everything. He must keep checking, obsessively. There was an enemy. A very, very clever enemy. He had to trap them. Are you ant or human, Paul? An ant goes insane.

'Workstation One?'

'*Inactive,*' said the patient Hunter.

'Workstation Three?'

'*Inactive.*'

He reviewed the progress of the message. It was still going out over the main transmitter. He checked the two auxiliary transmitters. They were silent.

He could not stand still.

'Continue to monitor all workstations,' he said. He rose to his feet, left his chamber and glided through the common room and the airlock beyond. He stopped at a door.

'Vandamme?'

There was no answer. He entered at once.

She had changed the wall displays. The desolation of the moon's surface was gone. The predominant colour was a rich blue, grading from darker colours to light. But at one point on the wall a small shape in luminous gold stood out like a flame, brightening all the blues around it into whites and golds. It had a very calm, almost sleepy effect. Faint music was coming from somewhere. Paul was reminded of the lights of stained-glass windows and the interiors of those once-holy places on Earth where almost no one went any more.

The door to her sleeping chamber was open. The chamber itself was empty, with all the personal clutter stowed away.

Vandamme was at her workstation, craning round at him. Her screen showed a view of the hangar with the suited figure of Lewis still poring over the dismantled harvester.

'What is he doing?' asked Paul.

'Just maintenance,' said Vandamme. 'It shouldn't take long.' She eyed him warily. 'What do you want?'

'Nothing,' said Paul curtly. 'May I watch?'

She was uneasy. That might be because he had marched in on her. It might be because they had parted so badly last time they had spoken.

But it might be for another reason.

'Do you want me to tell Lewis you're out?'

'Not yet. I may change my mind again.'

She did not turn back to the monitor. She was keeping her eyes on him. He stood there, balancing on his toes, and said nothing.

Suddenly she said, 'Would you like me to make you coffee?'

'Yes, if you want,' he answered, surprised.

'Just watch him for me, would you? You don't have to tell him it's you.'

She rose. Glancing at him once more, she left the chamber.

Immediately Paul took her place at the console. He said, 'Hunter.'

The face of the ape-man appeared.

'Report activity on all workstations.'

'*Workstations One and Three are inactive. Workstation Two is Hunter. Workstation Four, repeat of message zero eight: zero four: zer—*'

'Thank you. Kitchens?'

'*Increase of energy consumption by three kilowatts in the Bravo unit kitchen.*'

That would be Vandamme making the coffee. But she did not need to stand over it while it was brewing. She could have slipped into another chamber, even into his own. What was she doing?

186

He knew it was unreasonable. If she had been going to sabotage his transmission she would have done it here, before he turned up. And in the time it took to make coffee, what could she do? One burst at best. But he was in the realm of the unreasonable now. Any move by anyone must be suspected. Paranoia must be the worst of all madnesses – the ultimate loneliness. And he must act as if the madness were his. 'Main radio transmitter?'

'*Responding to Workstation Four – repeat of message zero eight: zero—*'

'Auxiliary transmitters?'

'*Inactive.*'

Vandamme was in the kitchen. Lewis was in the outer layers, and May . . . Where was May?

Vandamme was in the *Bravo* unit kitchen! She was in the living-quarter suite that Paul and May and Lewis inhabited. Why had she gone there, when there was an identical kitchen just opposite her own chamber in the Alfa suite?

Where was May?

'How do you like that?' said Lewis.

Paul sat bolt upright in shock. Voice shaking, he said, 'Hunter!' again. The ape appeared. But Paul could not speak. He did not know what instruction to give.

It shouldn't make any difference, he told himself. If Vandamme had gone to the Bravo unit so she could speak with May – it should make no difference. The monitors were all inactive. The auxiliary antennae were inactive. No one was interfering.

But where was May?

She should be on watch. Lewis must have shuffled the watches again. Why? Why had he done that? What were they up to?

'It's still a bit crooked,' came Lewis's voice over the monitor.

Paul jumped to his feet. So abrupt was his movement that in the light gravity he lifted off the floor and stumbled as he came down. He turned for the door of the chamber. It opened. Vandamme had returned with two covered mugs in her hand. 'It's strange that you came in just then,' she said. 'I was wondering about something you said, and whether I could ask you about it. When you wrote that about the We making the universe—'

'Wait!' he exclaimed, pushing past her.

'What's the matter?'

'Need to check something!'

'Don't you want your coffee?'

He skipped away, ignoring her. He passed the airlock. In the far common room he stopped in front of the seal to May's chamber.

'May?'

No answer.

'May!'

No answer.

He went in.

The room was dark but it brightened immediately on his entry. There was no one there. The monitor was unmanned. The screen was blank.

'May!' Paul shouted. He beat on the sleeping-chamber door. 'Are you there?'

A voice answered indistinctly from inside.

As he waited for the door to open, Paul had time to ask himself what he was doing, hammering here at May's bedroom. He had been surprised. Did that matter so much? There would be some explanation why the watches had changed again. But he couldn't think what it was. And the change was suspicious. Anything was suspicious . . .

The door opened. May stood there, dressed only in a sleeping shirt that dropped to her upper thighs. Her hair was tousled, her eyes small, her cheeks suffused with sleep.

'This had better be important,' she croaked.

He stared at her.

'What's the matter, Paul?' said May.

'I thought you were on watch,' he stammered.

'Vandamme agreed to stand in for me.'

'Why?'

'For God's sake – what business is that of yours, Paul?'

'*Why* did the watches change?'

She glared at him. 'Because pregnant people,' she said curtly, 'need to sleep.' She looked over his shoulder. Vandamme was standing in the door to the common room. She had followed him all the way from her chamber. She still held the two covered cups in her hand.

'What on Earth's going on?' cried May.

For a moment he stared at them both, feeling all the blood running to his face. Then he snarled, 'We're not on Earth,' and stalked past Vandamme to shut himself in his own chamber.

None of them had interfered. Lewis had been in the outer layers. May had been asleep – fast asleep, until he had come beating at her door. Vandamme had been monitoring Lewis and then making the coffee. She had made it in the Bravo unit because after ten years of use the Alfa kitchen devices were no longer reliable.

There was no one else – unless he counted the unborn child, curled in the warm blindness of May's womb.

And his signal had been jammed again.

Your 09:04:0124 Message corrupted. The following groups unreadable . . .

. . . Investigate and report.

'Hunter!'

'*Yes?*'

'Has someone tampered with you?

'*No.*'

'My message was corrupted. How was it done?'

'*I cannot answer this question.*'

'Someone's tampered with you!'

'*No.*'

'But what if you're wrong?'

The ape-man stared at him. No answer came.

'What if you are—?' began Paul again. Then he stopped himself. He looked into the blankness of the ape-man's expression. 'No, cancel that! Try again. There are four people on the station. Which of them were active between zero one-twenty and zero one-thirty yesterday?'

'*Records show that five people came to the station. One deceased at eleven: zero three: thirteen thirty-one: twenty fifty-seven. Two were on watch, one was off watch but active, and one off watch and inactive at the time you indicate.*'

'Stop.'

At the shoulders of the Hunter the concealing grasses

waved silently, like the heads of a crowd of people all on tiptoe.

'Say all that again.'

'*Records show that five people came to the station. One deceased at eleven: zero three: thirteen thirty-one: twenty fifty-seven—*'

'What if that's wrong?'

Again the ape-man stared at him blankly.

XIV

They could have done it, Paul thought.

They could have done it. They could have lied when they reported his death. He could be alive now. The station had three hundred per cent redundancy. There would be other living-quarter suites, besides the two he knew about. If Lewis was heating and pressurizing two suites, why not three? There could be sleeping chambers, furniture, even monitors. Lewis could instruct the conveyors to bring the man his food. He could have powered up a separate computer system and be doing everything relating to the extra man on that. No Hunter could leap from one system to another. *What do you know about how many people the station can hold?*

Lewis! Who had gone out to recover the body? Lewis had. Fake the death – on the screen the crew would see nothing but the suited body collapsing. Set up new chambers for the fugitive. Bury something man-shaped and say that it was the body. All possible. No one else need know, except Lewis – and Thorsten.

But – did Vandamme not know? Was it possible that her partner, and her colleague, could let her live for *nine years* in the station believing that she was alone?

Possible, yes.

But far, far more likely that she knew.

She did know. Her personality – that closed, praying, work-obsessed personality – was a lie. They had known, all four of them, that a new man was coming to the station. They had known that sooner or later he would want company. They had decided, together, how she would keep the newcomer at a distance while her partner hid. Paul had looked inside her sleeping chamber and seen it neat and tidy – so neat and tidy that perhaps she never slept there. And at the end of each watch she would slip through another airlock to spend the night in her living man's arms.

Then she was the biggest liar of all. *She* was the real enemy.

But why, why, why? Why fake a death? Why go that far?

Because . . .

It will think about how to get the World Ear to function out here after all, Lewis had said. And *This is the worst possible thing you could have done.*

To get the World Ear to function, Earth must understand the magnetic tail. It was data from the tail that was lost whenever there was interference. But the interference itself would seem suspicious. The obvious suspect would be the station telmex. Unless he was thought dead.

It was Thorsten who had suggested that the source was the field.

Could they have done it? Could they? Crazy, to think that a man might be willing to fake his death and spend the remainder of his life in hiding, living apart from the others like a ghost in the station! And condemn another man, who was happy in the World Ear and the warm air of Earth, to be transported out here to take his place? It was a mad thought – but was it he who was mad, or they? It would stay with him now. It would gnaw at him. It would drive him insane, just thinking about it. And when he looked at it, was it any more crazy than allowing himself to be exiled to the very edge of the solar system? Once the reasons *seem* good, who could say what a man might do?

He had eliminated everyone else.

It was not an accident.

It was not natural.

But if – just supposing – it were true? Just supposing there were not four people in the station but five – how would he prove it?

There were thousands of bubbles. Eliminate the Alfa and Bravo living quarters and the outer layers, which could only function as insulation, and there would be – well, at least a thousand still. How could he search through them all? Put on a suit and go out to look? They would soon see what he was doing. Lewis could deny him the permissions to pass certain seals, claiming that his behaviour was irrational. And who would blame Lewis for that?

Or worse, they could simply move Thorsten into chambers that Paul had already explored; pressurize them, depressurize the old ones and watch while Paul blundered on through the bubbles, searching for a man who had slipped through his fingers. He could live his life and die in this place and never know the truth.

Report to Earth?

But Earth *would* think he was mad! He could not risk that. Not yet. First he would have to build a stronger case. First, he would have to find out whether or not he was mad himself. And . . .

And there was a way.

There was one place where the man could not be.

XV

The display reflected inside his pressure-suit helmet read: *Ex: 0.6 Suit: 1.0 Temp: -80°.* He was back in the main hangar.

The lighting flickered on coldly, triggered by his movement. The rows of crawlers stood in their places. At the near end of one row was a harvester with its back wheels dismantled – the one that Lewis had been working on. It sat on its grounded rear axle like a big grey frog squatting on its haunches.

Paul skipped quickly down the aisle between the machines. He came to a halt before the red crawler.

'Power,' he said.

A yellow light flared on the crawler's roof.

'Open.'

The hatch opened. The interior was lit. He clambered up and inside.

'Close.'

He passed through the airlock and pulled himself along

to the pilot seats, trailing his legs in the minimal gravity. The screen came on automatically. So did the displays. He keyed in the pressurization sequence. Numbers on the screen and inside his helmet began to whirl. Gradually he became aware of sounds – the hiss of air, the hum of power.

The power indicator had started to fall: *98%*.

Ex: 1.0 Suit: 1.0 Temp: -12°.

The crawler was a little pressurized box. If he removed his helmet now he would be able to survive.

He did not remove his helmet. He called up the crawler command mode options and studied them. He chose *Full Manual Override.*

An alert appeared. Full Manual Override meant that the crawler could not be commanded remotely from the station. If the crawler driver became incapacitated, the station crew could not pilot him out of trouble.

Paul dismissed the alert.

The system demanded an authorization code. He gave his. The system accepted it. It trusted him, because he was the telmex. Communications were his responsibility.

He placed his feet on the pedals, his hand on the clumsy great joystick.

Forward.

The hum increased. The screen showed the seal at the far end of the hangar coming towards him. At this point in his trip with Vandamme they had turned to the right, into the first lichen bubble.

He kept the joystick pointed ahead.

The seal filled the screen. He lifted his foot to halt the crawler, found the *Open* key and pressed it. He piloted the crawler into the airlock.

Vandamme's voice spoke in his ear.

'Who's in the crawler?'

She must have seen him on her monitor. Maybe she had been about to take another of her search crawlers out.

'Munro? Is that you in the crawler?'

'. . . Yes.'

'Are you going outside?'

'I'm doing an inspection.'

'You should use a utility crawler for inspections outside.'

'This is better for what I have to do.'

Lewis could override any instructions he gave to the utility crawlers. He did not want to get halfway to his goal only to find his crawler turning back.

'We should have full crew if you are going outside.'

Full crew meant two people in the manned crawler, one piloting a utility crawler remotely to lead or follow, and one – Lewis – in overall command. And an outside mission should be conducted to a clear plan, with schedules, objectives and abort patterns all discussed and agreed beforehand. And Earth should be informed too.

'It's not necessary for this mission.'

The airlock had closed behind him. The numbers on the screen were tumbling again. He became aware of a faint creaking around him, running along the sides of the cabin like the steps of a huge but invisible spider. He wondered what it was.

The exterior temperature had reached -140°. It blinked and displayed *133K*. The creaking intensified. For an instant the temperature display wavered back to Celsius. Then it switched to Kelvin again, falling slowly to 129. The seal ahead of him opened. He drove forward into the first insulating layer.

It was unlit. He rotated the screen view. The lights of the crawler, rotating obediently on the roof, showed him a huge, featureless, arched tunnel, running to left and right and curving backwards as it ran. The view was misty. The gases that filled the tunnel were dense with the extreme cold. The seal to the next layer was ahead of him. He pressed the *Open* key. Nothing happened.

Cursing softly, he hit it again. Still nothing happened. He wondered if Vandamme had grown suspicious enough of what he was doing to override the crawler controls and lock the seal. But Vandamme should not have been able to do that. Only Lewis had the necessary permissions.

He had to get out, quickly! Once he was out, no one could stop him.

Think. Why doesn't an airlock open? Because the automatic systems pick up a danger of decompression. And the obvious danger of decompression was . . .

He rotated the view again. The seal behind him was still closing. That was all it had been. Calm down. He must calm down. He was not thinking clearly and he must. There was a long way to go.

There. Closed. Now hit the *Open* key. And forward. And wait, and wait and wait . . .

The airlock closed behind him. The readings began to tumble again. Again he heard that ominous creaking, filtering through his helmet. Now he understood what it was.

It was thermal. The synthetic hull of the crawler was contracting as the temperature dropped away. Normally it stood in a hangar heated to -80° Celsius. But in the space of a few short minutes it was being exposed to a savage change – over a hundred degrees. The crawler was actually shrinking in the grip of the cold.

Paul swallowed. His palms tingled. The display had reached 90K. The seal ahead of him was opening. He rolled forward.

Another featureless, curving tunnel; but a different shape. The chamber was shorter – he could see the end walls. The outer layer was the most exposed to impacts and failures, and so had more compartments for greater safety. It was thick with mist. The mist flickered with light, as if tiny, silent thunderstorms were playing somewhere in the chamber, out of view of the screen. The glow came and went and left everything in darkness. A few seconds later it came again. It was the aurora of the station – the action of charged particles from space colliding with the gases trapped in this outer protective layer. The atmosphere out here was not composed of oxygen but of nitrogen and ammonia. The pressure hovered around 0.3. Even so, at ninety degrees Kelvin the gases were on the verge of liquefying. Droplets glistened where his headlights fell on the far wall.

There was a small scattering of something on the floor to one side of the seal. Fragments of a glass-like material, he thought: the remains of May's ill-advised experiment. *She was showered with shards.* It would not have been glass. May would have known better than to use glass. There probably wasn't a single item made of glass in the whole of the station. Even so, the material had shattered under the stress of unequal interior and exterior pressures. If one of those shards had punctured her suit, she would have died as Thorsten was supposed to have died.

He had one more step to go.

The seal opened. He piloted the crawler forward

and waited. The seal before him was the door to the surface.

A voice spoke in his helmet. It was Lewis.

'Paul, do you hear me?'

'Yes.'

'Vandamme says you are going outside. Is that true?'

'Yes.'

He heard Lewis's intake of breath.

'I can't permit you to go outside. You are not properly crewed and neither are we. It isn't safe.'

'I'm going outside, Lewis. Don't try to stop me.'

'I will certainly stop you. You've given no justification for your actions. You're putting yourself at risk and also the station. We can't afford to lose you or the crawler. You must return at once.'

'I am not going far, Lewis.'

'What are you going to do?'

'I'm going to see Thorsten.'

There was a slight pause. Paul rotated the view. The air-lock seal behind him was still closing. Come *on*!

'Thorsten is dead, Paul,' said Lewis slowly. 'You can't see him.'

'Yes I can.'

A faint clicking of keys came over his earpiece.

'I'm overriding the systems, Paul. The outer door will not open. You must return and explain yourself.'

'No.'

'You can't go out, Paul!'

The airlock had closed. The numbers began to tumble once more.

'Open the door, Lewis.'

'I am not going to—'

'Open it!'

'I'll damn well do nothing of the sort. You're acting irrationally . . .'

'Open it, damn you!'

'. . . danger to yourself and to us. You can sit there as long as you like—'

'*Lewis!*'

Furiously Paul punched the key marked *Bore*. Something clicked faintly above his head. His screen showed another view – the outer door again, but this time looking down a long mechanical arm.

'Open it – or I'll break it down!'

There was a pause.

'You can't do that,' said Lewis. 'You'll break the bore, more likely.'

'Shall we see?'

He jerked the joystick. Clumsily the arm reached forward, like a long finger.

'Paul, if you touch that door we'll restrain you when you

get back in.'

'You're going to open it, Lewis! You're going to open it *now*!'

Through the fabric of the crawler, through the layer of his suit, he felt the *clunk* as the bore-nose came to rest against the rim of the door. There would be four bolts, he calculated. Maybe five.

He pressed *Start*. Slowly the bore began to turn. In utter silence dust began to fly.

There was a muttered curse in his ear. Other voices, more distant, were speaking in alarm. They must all have gathered around the console . . . *When Lewis called us into his work-chamber . . . He had Thorsten on his monitor . . . There was something odd about Thorsten's answers . . .*

A thin stream of shavings was dropping to the floor.

'All right! Paul, all right! Stop the bore! I'm releasing it!'

Paul jerked the joystick backwards. The arm recoiled. The drill was still spinning. He stopped it.

The last door was opening. He pressed the pedal. The crawler rolled forward, out onto the permanent ice.

The first thing was the gleam of something like water in the crawler lights. Like water? It probably *was* water, mixed with liquid nitrogen and ammonia, which kept it from freezing even as it seeped through the appalling cold of the crust and broke out through some vent in the surface. He could not see the vent itself. It might even be under the station. The station was designed to float on such flows.

The second thing was the change in the crawler's motion. Its wheels were on an uneven surface. After the smooth floors of the station it was juddering, even bouncing in a slow, uneasy rhythm that reminded him of being in a boat. The engine was powerful, the gravity low. The wheels were splayed wide to prevent it from overturning. Even so, it would not be difficult to roll it. And that would be disaster.

If the crawler rolled he would be stuck, even if the hatch would still open. The temperature stood at 36K. Thirty-six degrees above absolute zero. *The ground out there is trying to suck your heat out through your boots.*

His foot had lifted automatically from the accelerator. The bouncing motion eased. The crawler came to a halt just short of the pool's edge. How deep would it be? No knowing.

He rotated the screen.

The floor of the canyon gleamed faintly with ice and pools, all bathed in a faint light like the last half-hour of twilight back on Earth, before the true night set in. The light would be coming from overhead, from the distant, star-like Sun. There would be more light once he got out of the canyon. Here, everything was enveloped in the shadowy walls of ice that rose above him.

The screen did not seem to do an upward view. Without it he felt very blind.

His lights showed him tracks in the ice, leading away to his left along the edge of the liquid flow. They would have been made by the utility crawlers. Crawlers went out from the station on various missions, but most involved climbing up the side of the canyon, up the natural ledge towards Thorsten's cairn.

He moved the joystick and pressed gingerly on the pedal. The crawler lurched forward, swinging to follow the tracks. As long as he stayed in the tracks his chances of getting stuck or overturning were far less.

And his chance of coming back safely was far greater.

'Paul?'

It was May's voice.

'Hello.'

'Paul, what are you doing? Please tell us.'

You talk to him, they would have said to her. *Maybe he'll listen to you. You try.*

'I'm going to see Thorsten.'

'Paul, we don't understand! Why?'

'Because there must be someone else!'

Pause. He could imagine the crew members looking at one another down in the station. Wondering, frightened . . . *He's mad*, they would be thinking. *He's gone mad.*

And Lewis? Had he understood yet what it was that Paul had guessed? What was he thinking now? And what would he say to the others?

Would he give in, as he had given in at the door?

But even if he did, Paul would not believe him. He could confess the truth now, then later he would claim he had only said it to get Paul back inside the station. There was just one way to be sure.

'Paul?'

It was May again. There was a tremble in her voice.

'Paul – please. Whatever you are going to do, you have to come back. You understand? Please.'

She thought he was going to kill himself.

'I'll come back.'

'Paul. Please come back *now*. If you have an accident we'll lose you, and the crawler as well!'

'I'm going to see Thorsten.'

Silence.

The crawler had begun to climb. To his left was the ice wall. To his right, a drop. The way was narrow – comfortable enough for utility crawlers but not for the big red crawler. He was hugging the cliff as closely as possible.

It was steep too. It was far steeper than such a road on Earth would have been. Of course there was less gravity to combat, but at the same time it made the risk of overturning seem greater. It was mostly natural, the crew had said. The constructors had only had to improve it. Improve it? What did that mean? Pile rubble into the cracks, he supposed. They hadn't had much choice about its course – or its width.

'Damn!'

'Paul, what happened?' That was Lewis, tense. They must be following his every move down there.

'It's just narrow!'

'Paul, you mustn't take this kind of risk! Come back now. If you like we'll pilot a utility up there—'

'The hell with that!'

He had never used the word *hell* before. He had an idea that it was supposed to be a very hot place. Bitterly, he laughed aloud.

'Paul. We do not understand. Tell us why you are doing this!'

'Because there must be someone else! There must be! And it has to be Thorsten.'

There was silence for a moment. Paul supposed they were digesting what he had said, absorbing it, understanding his accusation. And then they would deny it.

But what Lewis said was: 'Paul, repeat that last, please. You broke up. It has to be . . . ?'

'Get out of my ear, Lewis!'

'Paul, you must help us!'

'Get out of my ear and let me drive this thing! *Damn!*'

For one horrible moment he thought a wheel was spinning in empty space. But the crawler lurched onwards, upwards. He could see the rim of the canyon, ahead and above him. Two, three hundred metres? Impossible to tell. The sky was nearly as black as the ice. Only the gleam on the canyon rim showed him where it might be. And the shape of a spar, catching the light.

The way was widening. It was becoming a slope of ice – luminous, fissured ice. The big wheels bounced but maintained their grip. He was getting more used to this. His power indicator read *67%*.

The cairn was a little way ahead of him, set back from the natural line of advance, just as if it were an old roadside shrine on Earth. It was built of debris from the station, coated over the years with thin layers of frost. If it had not been for the spar planted in its cone it would have been just one more icy hummock in all that waste of ice, silvered with the thin ammonia frost that fell from the sky.

The crawler heaved itself up to the ridge beside the cairn.

Brake. Lower and lock the legs.

Legs locked, said the screen.

And look around, because he might never come out here

again. Slowly he rotated the camera. The images traversed his screen.

He was looking across ridge after ridge of ice, dark where it fell steeply and silver-purple where the light fell upon it. The sky was a dull blue-black, streaked here and there with thin greys. As the camera turned, Paul saw a man-made radio antenna, sited about half a kilometre away. That was one of the auxiliaries. Its dish was pointed to the sky.

And now other things were coming into view: the edge of the canyon, frighteningly close and deep, it seemed. The screen would not look down into it, just as it would not show him the planet overhead. And what was that? Another man-made structure, a little along the canyon edge. It stood like a radio antenna, with some kind of dish pointing to the sky. But it was not an antenna. And the angle of the dish was curious.

There was another one beyond it. And another. There was a long row of them on the lip of the canyon. And there were more on the far side, again with their angled dishes . . . Yes, those were the outer ring of the Sun-gathering system, tilting their mirrors to spill the weak rays down into the bottom of the canyon where the secondary and tertiary mirrors would focus them onto the baths of algae below the insulating layers of the station. Plus twelve Celsius, the temperature had been down there, in the glare gathered from forty-eight huge mirrors combined.

The display on his screen read *37K*.

Now the screen was completing its tour, looking up the length of the canyon along another line of standing mirrors to where the cone of 'Humperdinck' heaved itself into view in the background. And here, sliding into view again before him, was the cairn of rubble with the pylon poking up out of the top of it. The feature the station crew called 'Thorsten'.

That's Thorsten, he had heard one of them say. Who had it been? He remembered it as May's voice. Did May really believe that Thorsten lay out here?

Paul did not believe it.

'We'll see,' he said. And he began to pick at the controls.

Down in the station he had studied the crawler plans carefully. It was equipped with all the main instruments available on a utility – arm camera for close inspections, de-icer, grips and a bore. He switched the display to the arm camera and inspected the rubble of which the cairn was made.

The shapes were small and mostly regular. They must have been waste containers and debris left over from the construction, carted up here by patient utilities to make this pile. That had been nine years ago. The layer of frost on them was far thinner than on the landscape. Even so, it was enough to have fused them together in a single lump. He had been expecting that.

He selected the de-icer and guided it forward, pulling back the camera at the same time to watch what he was doing. The nozzle hovered centimetres from one of the boulders. He pressed *Activate*.

The de-icer was loaded with nitrogen, heated within the crawler to a few degrees below zero Celsius. The frost melted instantly under the blast of gas. A puff of fine granules flew silently in all directions – that was the nitrogen, rebounding from its target and freezing even as it flew. On the display the battery indicator was falling faster: *63 . . . 62 . . . 61*. Paul kept the blast of gas aimed on one irregular piece, which might have been a lump of old foam covered in ice.

And it split. A piece rolled gently down the side of the cairn. Around it, the other fragments stayed where they were, still frozen into place.

Paul shifted his target.

'Munro!' It was Vandamme's voice, urgent and upset. 'What are you doing? Leave him alone!'

He frowned and looked at the controls in front of him. Down in the station they must have tuned their screens to his. They could see everything he could. They could see him violating their shrine. He looked for a way of blocking them out, but he did not know how.

On the other hand, they could do nothing to stop him. Not now.

He moved the de-icer to another piece.

'Paul – that's Thorsten's grave! Please leave him alone!'

'He's not there, May.' It was a shrine but it was also a lie.
Soon he would prove that.

'Paul, I don't understand. What do you mean?'

'There has to be someone else! In the station. If he's in the
station, he can't be here.'

'Paul, I can't hear you. I can't hear what you are saying!
But if you can hear me, please, please leave him alone!'

He could hear her perfectly clearly. What was the matter?

'I said there has to be someone else!'

No answer. On the screen, rubble fell from the side of the
cairn in a long, silent cascade. Fragments bounced lazily
outwards and disappeared from view. The pylon was
leaning drunkenly. At its foot he glimpsed some sort of
wrapping.

He clenched his teeth. Could he be wrong, after all?

But if Lewis had been acting alone, he would have to have
buried something. The others would have seen him doing it.
There would have to have been something that was
'Thorsten' to lay at the foot of the pylon.

In his ear, Lewis spoke.

'Paul, can you hear me?'

Paul ignored him. He activated the grip and brought it in
to prise a lump free. More lumps tumbled, hiding whatever

214

it had been from view. The pylon tipped and fell lazily to the surface.

'Paul – you are breaking up. What is your battery reading?'

Paul checked it.

'Fifty-four per cent.'

There was a pause.

'Paul, your signals aren't reaching us. Maybe your power is faulty. Maybe the indicator is wrong. You must come back now.'

(A last, desperate effort, Lewis! But how calm you keep your voice.)

'Paul! You understand – if you run out of power up there, there's nothing we can do. Nothing.'

'I won't run out of power.'

Although it was getting close. He had used half of what he had. He still had the journey back to come. And the cairn was being awkward. The lumps of material kept getting in the way – falling and lying where he didn't want them to. It was incredibly slow and clumsy, to pick them up one at a time, swing the grip arm and drop them somewhere to one side. He could see the wrapping. It looked like a standard vacuum coating sealed around a long, indistinct object that might have been the body of a man. He had nothing to cut the wrapping with. For a moment he thought he was going to have to pick it up in the grips and carry the thing all the way back down to the station. But he hunted along the length of it with the camera, and at one end – it might have been the head – he found a flap where the coating had been sealed together. He brought the grip arm over.

'Please,' whispered Erin Vandamme.

He almost stopped then. He almost stopped for her, because of the pity and distress in her voice. He gritted his teeth. Remorselessly, the arm took hold of the flap in the vacuum coating.

'Paul! Stop!'

He lifted the arm, dragging the wrapped object with it. It came all of a piece and for a moment he knew a fierce rush of triumph. Then he realized that even if it was a human body it would be frozen absolutely stiff and would not bend at the waist or anywhere.

'Paul!' May, still pleading. But it was too late. The coating was tearing even before he was ready for it. Slowly, silently, it ripped away like a mask. A voice – either May or Vandamme – cried aloud in Paul's ear.

And his screen was filled with a face.

A dead face in a shroud of vacuum coating, diminishing as it fell to its bed of frozen debris.

Drifting away, drifting down to the ground . . .

The scalp was nearly bald, the brow wrinkled, the skin

white. The eyes were open. They ignored Paul, sitting sheltered in his crawler. Frozen in that hellish place, they stared at the empty sky. Around the mouth the lips curled back to show the teeth, in a fierce, desperate grimace, as if the man still looked down the long tunnel of death and saw no end.

Thorsten Bondevik, who had died nine years ago.

The body touched the rubble. For an instant the face seemed to rise back towards the camera, so that Paul's heart lurched and he thought the dead man was actually lifting his head as he lay.

And then it burst into a fountain of crystals.

'Damn!' whispered Paul. 'Oh damn!'

The little shimmering cloud cleared slowly, drifting to rest upon the shoulders and mutilated head. The body of the dead man had shattered to icy rubble within its protective sheeting. Where the face had been there was only an indistinct pile of crystals and torn fabric. Brittle in the extreme cold, without even the light pressure of its protective bag, there had been nothing to hold it together any more.

'Sorry,' Paul groaned.

Then he said: 'Sorry, Van. I was wrong.'

'She's gone, Paul,' said Lewis harshly. 'They both have. They went when you smashed him to pieces.'

Paul swore.

In the little cabin of the crawler, high in the hellish wastes of that world so far from Earth, he put his head in his hands.

'Paul?' said Lewis at last. 'Paul!'

'Yes?'

'Are you coming back now? Or are you going to stay out there with him?'

Paul looked at the screen. The camera had wandered a little. It showed a view of scattered rubble, the end of the fallen pylon and the dead man's feet.

'Paul!'

'I'm coming.'

'Thank God for that much. What's your power reading?'

Paul looked at it.

'Thirty-eight per cent,' he said hollowly.

'That's what I was afraid of,' said Lewis grimly.

Paul looked at the screen again. 'I can't just leave him like this.'

'For God's sake! Yes, you can! Get yourself back here *now*!'

Obstinately Paul jabbed at the controls. The grip arm was still holding the flap of coating, like an old man who had taken out a handkerchief and then forgotten what he had in his fingers. He swung it slowly over the corpse and released it. It fell across the dead man's broken waist. He lowered the arm and dragged the thing clumsily over the remains of the head. He felt he should do better than that, even though nothing he could do would ever make up for what he had already done.

But there was no time. Even as he watched the screen, his battery display dropped again. He must go.

Tune the screen to the main viewer. Fold and lock limbs. Unlock and withdraw legs.

Joystick, and pedals.

Power: 36%.

He turned the crawler. He knew that even this manoeuvre was a waste of energy, and yet he did not dare attempt the narrow cliff track in reverse. He pointed the crawler downhill and nudged it forward. He felt it tilt its nose downwards. The way was steep. It seemed much steeper than he remembered it coming up.

And there was nothing to draw him on now. There was no hunt, because there was no quarry. He had been wrong, wrong all the time. The man lay dead on the horrible waste behind him. There was only the taste of failure.

'Paul?'

'Yes.'

'Take it steadily. If you rush it on that path you'll tip yourself.'

'I know.'

'I'm sending a crawler up to lead you in.'

Paul knew he should say *Thank you*. But shame made the words stick and he did not speak them.

Down, now. The narrow, gloomy path that wasn't a path, just a ledge-like crack down the face of the cliff. He could feel his body wanting to fall slowly forward with the slope, held into place only by his seat straps. Ice glowed in his lights just metres ahead of his vehicle. Beyond that was darkness. To his left was the drop. To his right was the ice wall.

He concentrated fiercely on the path, nudging his crawler again and again into the cliff until he could feel and hear the ice scraping along the hubs of his wheels. He was aware from time to time of the shapes of the station below him, glimpsed in the middle distance: a huge mound of frosted curves, unnatural in this jagged landscape, mounted by all kinds of slender structures. He was aware of the flash of a secondary mirror, directing captured sunlight up into its tertiary. But he did not dare look. Nor did he look at the floor of the cavern, gleaming with flows of freezing liquids. He crept on downwards. It was slow. It seemed far slower than his outward journey. The crawler rolled sickeningly and its outer wheels spun and slipped on the edge. Again he nudged it in towards the cliff wall. He felt the inner wheels scrape. Had the path got narrower since he had come up? Had some of it fallen away under his wheels as he climbed?

Power: 25%.

His teeth were set, his lips bared like those of the corpse he had smashed on the clifftop. And still the way led downwards. And still the canyon floor was no nearer. Time to pray, he thought.

Time to pray, but he knew no prayers. Dimly he remembered the voice of Erin Vandamme chanting about waters and green pastures. But that was wrong. Worse, here, than it had been even in the station. He remembered there had been words in her prayer about paths and about the shadow of death. *For You are with me*, she had written. But there was no one with him. Not here. There couldn't be. Maybe back in the station she was praying for him. She had said she didn't stop praying until whoever went out came back. But there was no one with him here.

And more likely she was weeping in her room – weeping over what he had done.

Lights on the path ahead of him!

Gone. But now there they were again. Lights! Two little beady lights, about a hundred metres off. Not the miraculous glow of some angel but the headlights of one of the little utility crawlers, hurrying up the fissure towards him.

'Paul?'

'Yes?'

'I've got you on my screen. Can you see me?'

Lewis didn't mean *me*. He meant *the crawler I have sent out to you*. But, yes, suddenly it was like having company on the road.

'Yes I can.'

He could see its body now, gleaming yellow behind its lights. It had stopped. He braked too. The two crawlers sat on the ledge looking at each other, like insects that had met in a crack in a wall.

'Right,' said Lewis's voice. 'What's your power reading?'

Paul had not been looking at the power. Very determinedly, he had not been looking at it. Now he did.

'Twelve.'

'Twelve! You're sure?'

'Yes.'

'God!' Lewis broke off. Then he said: 'I'm afraid . . .'

In the silence, Paul heard the coming of his own death.

'Paul?'

His throat was dry. 'Yes?'

'You'll have to depressurize the cabin.'

'I'll freeze!'

'Not at once. The only conduction will be through the wheels. The suit should keep you safe.'

The suit should keep you safe. Lewis was telling him to let the terrible cold into the crawler, to rely only on his suit, in order to lighten the demand on his power pack. And neither

222

of them knew how long he could safely do it for. And neither of them knew how much power it would save.

Some, surely.

Fingers trembling, he punched the controls. He watched the figures tumble.

'Done,' he said.

'How do you feel?'

Stupid question! *'Shit! Like shit!'*

'Follow me, then.'

He did not turn the utility crawler on that narrow ledge. He simply backed it. Paul saw its lights receding and followed them. They were a help. They let him anticipate what the path was going to do: how it was going to twist or narrow, before his own lights picked it out. Anticipation. That was the key. The brain could work so much faster if it could anticipate what was coming. Work faster, go faster.

He wished Lewis *would* go faster! Surely he could drive his crawlers faster than this! But the little utility was barely creeping down the slope ahead. Maybe Lewis was doing it deliberately – to force Paul to be careful. Speed would make no difference now. With the life-support systems off, the main drain on the crawler's power pack would be its speed. And the main danger, apart from running out of power, would be if Paul overturned or tumbled down the cliff. It did not matter what happened to the utility. There were other utilities. There was no other manned crawler. And there was no other Paul.

'I can see the valley floor,' said Lewis.

Paul said nothing.

'Paul – are you still all right?'

'So far.'

He knew he was feeling cold. There was a heaviness in his limbs. His seat hurt. His feet were going numb. But his brain still seemed to be working – for now.

'Follow me – there's a flow.'

Paul was still negotiating the last stretch of the descent. But Lewis hadn't waited. He was already guiding his crawler away, tracking first in towards the canyon wall and then away again, skirting the gleam of liquid that welled from within the moon's crust. Paul hurried after him. The curved dome of the station loomed ahead. He did not look at the battery reading.

'I've opened the airlock. Can you see it?'

A round hole. It looked the size of a mouse hole in that huge, smooth side. Blackness within.

'Yes.'

'Drive straight in. Don't stop. Don't wait for my crawler. I'm parking it.'

If he stopped now, he might never start again.

The yellow utility crawler veered abruptly off to his right. As he passed it, its lights died.

In, straight in. The hole of the airlock was ahead of him. Don't look at the display.

The screen brightened suddenly as the automatic lights came on. The motion of the crawler changed, no longer bumping but smooth with the floor of the station beneath his wheels. Inside the airlock he kept the crawler creeping forward all the time the outer doors were closing, fearing that the strain of starting from standstill would be too much for the depleted battery. He was almost touching the inner doors by the time they opened. And now the exterior temperature had begun to climb, all the way up to 90K. And on the floor of the tunnel compartment lay the shards of May's light-hearted experiment with the flask of air.

By the time he docked the crawler, the power display read 4%.

'Lewis? I'm in the hangar.'

'Good. You can reconnect the thing to charge. And then get yourself back to your quarters. I don't want to see you. Neither does anyone else.'

The silence after he broke the link was like a corpse tumbling gently in a low gravity field.

XVI

Shortly after his return, his monitor beeped. It showed him Hunter, emerging from a background of savannah grasses. Angrily Paul blanked the screen. He did not want to talk to Hunter.

He was not asked to perform any watches. He was not trusted with anything. He stayed in his quarters. If he ventured out for food, he did so when he thought the others were asleep or busy. If he heard them in the common room, or the kitchen area, he retreated behind his door again. He would rather starve a little than look into their eyes.

He had been wrong. Thorsten was dead. The man was dead and smashed to pieces, up there on the surface of the planet where no life would ever come. It had been crazy to think that he might somehow still be alive, haunting the station and the transmissions to Earth. Paul had known it was crazy, but still he had followed it because it was all he had left. He had wrenched the frozen body from its rest as if it had been a piece of garbage. In the process he had nearly lost himself and the manned crawler too.

How could he have been so wrong?

And how could he have been so stupid?

He had missed something. Somewhere back in his search, something had slipped past him—

'Paul?'

It was May, calling at his door. He did not want to talk to May. He did not want to talk to anyone. They were not supposed to be talking to him and for the moment that suited him.

'Paul? May I come in?'

'No.'

Silence.

He had missed something. What? It was not an accident, it was not a program, whether faulty or deliberate. It was not Lewis, or Vandamme or May. And it was not Thorsten.

What had he missed?

He should go on searching. He could be searching now. But he did not know where to look.

He could look at the Knowledge Store but he did not want to. They would have recorded his excursion. They would have commented on it: undertaken with inadequate supervision or backup, with no planning and to no purpose. Disciplinary action pending. They might even have added some of their own reactions. *Paul! Please leave him alone!*

He switched on the display of his monitor anyway. There was nothing else to do. And Hunter was still there, looking out of the screen with the blue sky and tall yellow grasses at his back.

'What do you want?' Paul snarled at him.

'*I have found a record showing evidence of intelligent interference.*'

'Have you?' Paul sank into his chair. (On Earth, he would have come down with a bump. But here, of course . . .) 'Couldn't you have told me earlier?'

'*I have been waiting to tell you.*'

'Earlier than yesterday, I mean!'

'*The record was not created before yesterday.*'

Paul tensed. Yesterday he had been out on the surface of the planet.

'Who was the source of interference?'

'*I do not know.*'

Useless!

'All right,' he sighed. 'Where was it coming from?'

'*From outside the station.*'

'I meant, which antenna? The main, or one of the auxiliaries?'

'*None of them.*'

Not from an antenna?

'A crawler, then?'

'*Not from any recognized station equipment.*'

'Show me the record.'

The screen blinked. The face of Hunter was replaced by a jumble of words.

It took Paul a long second to realize what he was looking at.

Who's in the crawler. Munro. Is that you in the crawler. Yes. Are you going outside. I'm doing an inspection. You should use a utility crawler for inspections outside. This is better for what I have to do. We should have full crew if you are going outside. It's not necessary for this mission.

Paul do you hear me. Yes. Vandamme says you are going outside. Is that true. Yes. I can't permit you to go outside. You are not properly crewed and neither are we. It isn't safe. I'm going outside Lewis. Don't try to stop me. I will certainly stop you. You've given no justification for your actions. You're putting yourself at risk and also the station. We can't afford to lose you or the crawler. You must return at once. I am not going far Lewis. What are you going to do. I'm going to see Thorsten . . .

'All right,' he sighed. 'What are you saying is intelligent interference?'

He was thinking that if Hunter said '*Your actions*' or

229

'*Leaving the station without permission,*' he would tell the thing that no, that had been *un*intelligent interference. There was no way that a computer program could be made to suffer. But at least he would have confused it.

'*The improving ability to anticipate the target phrase demonstrates that the source has the capacity to learn.*'

Target phrase?

He scanned down the passionless lines.

Paul. We do not understand. Tell us why you are doing this. Because there must be someone else. There must be. And it has to be ?????????? Paul repeat that last please. You broke up. It has to be. Get out of my ear Lewis. Paul you must help us. Get out of my ear and let me drive this thing. Damn. We'll see. Munro. What are you doing. Leave him alone. Paul that's Thorsten's grave. Please leave him alone. He's not there May. Paul I don't understand. What do you mean. There has to be someone ??????????????????? Paul I can't hear you. I can't hear what you are saying. But if you can hear me please please leave him alone. I said there has to be ????????????? Paul can you hear me. Paul you are breaking up. What is your battery reading. Fifty-four per cent. Paul your signals aren't reaching us. Maybe your power is faulty. Maybe the indicator is wrong. You must come back now. Paul.

He wanted to stop reading but he could not. There, spelled out on the screen in silence, was what had happened next.

You understand if you run out of power out there there's nothing we can do. Nothing. I won't run out of power. Please. Paul. Stop. Paul. Damn. Oh damn. Sorry. Sorry Van. I was wrong. She's gone Paul. They both have. They went when you smashed him to pieces.

'Paul?'
It was May again, back at his door. God! Why now?
'Paul, are you all right?'
'Yes, I'm all right.'
'Can I come in?'
'No!'
Then he added: 'Sorry, May.'
'I want to be sure you're all right.'
'I'm all right!'
Silence.
He found that he had shut his eyes – screwed them up and hunched his shoulders, like a child weeping in the corner of a room and refusing to be comforted.

He opened them. The words were still there on the screen before him.

. . . Because there must be someone else. There must be. And it has to be ????????? Paul repeat that last . . .

And:

What do you mean. There has to be someone ?????????????????? Paul I can't hear you. I can't hear what you are saying. But if you can hear me please please leave him alone. I said there has to be ???????????? Paul can you hear me.

'That's it?' he said. 'Those three groups?'

'*The improving ability to anticipate the target phrase demonstrates that the source has the capacity to learn,*' said Hunter.

'You're a machine all right. That's exactly what you said a moment ago.'

'*Thank you.*'

Paul peered at the broken message.

'Didn't I use that phrase earlier?'

He scrolled back.

Paul. Hello. Paul what are you doing. Please tell us. I'm going to see Thorsten. Paul we don't understand. Why. Because there must be someone else. Paul. Paul please. Whatever you are going to do you have to come back . . .

'Why wasn't that jammed, if the others were?'

'*The phrase will not have been anticipated prior to its first use.*'

No. It would not have been. Not if the interference was intelligent rather than automatic. First it had to be alerted. It had to recognize the possibility that the phrase might be transmitted. Only then could it begin to anticipate the use. And to improve its reactions each time.

'It's a radio signal?' he murmured.

'*It is a surge of charged particles affecting the radio signal.*'

'Charged particles? In the magnetic field?'

'*Yes.*'

Paul looked up at the display on the ceiling of his bubble.

There it was, as it always was and always would be to the end of his life. The thin crescent of the planet, spanning ten degrees of arc overhead, framed within the shadowed lips of the cliffs, with the Sun poised over it like a diamond on a half-ring.

'My God!' he whispered.

Then he said: 'I didn't mean that.'

'Paul?'

She was back again, at his door. He sat up. Dazedly his thoughts recovered themselves from the paths they had been chasing for so long.

Long? How long?

Hours, perhaps. They had been going round and round and round. Round and round a conclusion that was impossible and yet inevitable, like debris orbiting a planet, neither escaping from its field nor falling to a new home in the bosom of its earth.

'Paul!'

'Yes?' he said.

'May I – may I come in?'

He gripped the back of his chair. His eyes were focused on nothing.

'Yes,' he said. 'For God's sake – yes!'

There was a moment's hesitation. Then the seal opened.

It was not May. He had thought it must be May because she had called him 'Paul'. It wasn't.

It was Erin Vandamme, floating through his doorway towards him, and her eyes widened as she saw how his face was working. And he was not conscious of stepping towards her but he must have done, because they came together in mid-air, spinning gently with the force of the collision, and might have stumbled if they had not already been holding onto one another, holding fast, fast, with her arms around his chest and his face buried in her shoulder. His throat was tight and his eyes were weeping hot tears.

'I don't know who it is,' he cried. '*I don't know who it is!*'

XVII

'Paul!' she said. 'Stop . . . Do you hear me? I want you to take a breath. Deep breath, now. That's right – now do it again . . . All right . . .

'Now, slowly. Tell me. You don't know who what is?'

Trembling, he showed her Hunter's transcript. And again she made him stop, take breaths and repeat himself, as he stood at her shoulder jabbing his finger at the obliterated phrases.

'Wait. What are you saying has happened to these messages?'

'They've been jammed! Like the others!'

'Which others?'

'The tail data to Earth. Over the radio.'

'But that's a natural phenomenon.'

'*This* isn't natural. Look at it. It anticipates the words! That's *learning*!'

'So . . . who are you saying did it?'

'Someone else! I thought it must be Thorsten. But it wasn't! It's someone else.'

'You really thought Thorsten might not be dead?'

She hadn't looked at him. Her eyes were still on the screen, but she was not seeing it. The signals of her optic nerves were being suppressed. Her body was still. Her mind had focused inwards, turning over what he had said, trying to imagine how it could have seemed true. She was trying to understand how he could possibly have done what he had done.

'I knew it wasn't any of you. Thorsten was the only one left.'

She sighed. 'And I've known that he's dead. I've known it for nine years, as solidly as anything I could touch. To hear you saying you were going to see him – I thought the bottom had dropped out of my heart.'

She was silent for a while, looking at the screen where the bald words told the story of Paul's ride in the crawler.

'It wasn't any of us,' she said at length.

Then she asked carefully, 'Could it have been you?'

'No!'

'I need to be sure of that.'

'It wasn't me! I was going up to the cairn. I didn't want that conversation at all!'

'But the mind can trick itself, can't it? Especially if it's having difficulty relating to new surroundings. You could have muddled your own message and blanked your memory of doing so. You've been having a stressful time—'

'I'm not mad!'

'We're all a little mad. How could we not be – out here?'

She was studying columns of figures on the screen. Paul recognized them at once. They were the readings of activity in the magnetic field.

'I mean, we're all affected by being here,' she said. 'Like having vertigo. Balancing on the top of a tower that men have built to the stars. Like Babel. God saw what men did at Babel and he twisted their tongues so that they could no longer speak to one another. That was madness, of a sort.'

'I am *not mad*!'

She pressed another key. More figures filled the screen. Paul sank into the spare seating beside her.

'I am sorry for what I did to Thorsten,' he said.

She shook her head. 'He felt nothing. He was all frozen.'

Then she made a little sound, like a hiccup or a giggle cut short. She added, 'Like me.'

'You are not frozen.'

(She had come to his door. She had called him 'Paul'. A moment ago she had taken him in her arms.)

'Do you know what I felt when he was in his illness?'

'No.'

'I thought you did. I thought you would throw it at me.'

Paul frowned. 'What did you feel?'

'Nothing,' she sighed. 'Almost nothing. I still don't understand why. It was too difficult. It was too hard to reach him. Sometimes I was just angry. I still am. Why did we fail when the other two didn't? I don't know. But I know that I felt less than I should. Maybe I was protecting myself from what was happening to him. Only – when I thought you were going to do the same, suddenly it all came up. It was too much. I almost couldn't breathe.'

'You thought I would do what he did? Is that why you've come now?'

She looked at him. 'I came,' she said, 'because I missed you.'

She turned back to the screen. *Click*. The columns changed again. Like the landscapes of the moon they changed and changed and were always the same.

'Thank you,' said Paul.

Click. More numbers.

'That's today,' she murmured. 'And you were outside the station – when?'

'Yesterday – your watch. Eleven zero four . . .'

Once more she clicked the controls. Paul could see at once that the strings of figures were longer. But what spoke most clearly of all was her sudden stillness as she stared at the screen.

'All right,' she whispered at last. 'Let's be scientists now, shall we?'

'What do you want to do?'

'Repeat the experiment.'

Power: 92%.

Once again he was in the cabin of the crawler. Lewis was beside him. The screen showed a view of a liquid flow on the floor of the canyon – brilliant white in the headlights, ghostly blue when he rotated the screen away towards the shadow of the cliff walls. He was tense. He could feel his jaw clamped shut, his stomach tingling, how he kept fidgeting like a helpless bystander expecting the worst. His eyes flicked along the display, watching the figures for the tiniest change.

In the helmet: *Ex: 1.0 Suit: 1.0 Temp: -12°.*

On the crawler screen: *Ex: 0.01 Temp: 36K.* More than two hundred degrees separated the interior temperature of the crawler from that of the ground on which it stood. Paul could still hear the occasional creak of thermal stress from its fabric.

Power: 92%.

On the rear view the screen showed the station wall, curving up and away from them. They were too close to see the whole of it, or the structures that sprouted from its roof to gather sunlight and signals. The seal behind them had closed but Paul could still see the outline of it and the clear runs of crawler tracks that led to the door. It was less than a hundred metres away. Even so . . .

'Is this far enough?' said Lewis curtly.

They were the first words that he had spoken to Paul for six days.

'I hope so.'

'Get on with it, then.'

'May?' said Paul. 'Can you hear me?'

'We can hear you,' said May's voice in his helmet.

'Is Vandamme with you?'

'Yes.'

'Then listen to this. I think there is someone else with us out here. I don't know who or what they are but I know it's not one of us. It has to be someone else. I repeat, from the evidence I have, I think there is someone else with us out here. There's one, two, three, four of us, and there must be someone else.'

He stopped. He wondered if he had said enough. Perhaps he should have made it longer, padded it out, told them memories of Earth and things that were nothing to do with this place, and perhaps devised a sentence using the words *someone else* in a different context. Perhaps . . .

'Did you get that?' asked Lewis.

Lewis had not believed him. To begin with he had refused point blank to agree to another crawler expedition. Only

240

when Vandamme had managed to persuade May did he begin to listen. And he had taken his place in the crawler only because he trusted no one else to make sure that Paul was not interfering with his own signal. If this experiment failed there would be no more reasoning with him.

'Did you get it?' he repeated.

The silence lengthened. Then: 'We got it.'

That was May. There was something odd about her voice.

'Do you want us to try another location?'

'No. You can come back in.'

'You're sure? We could go a kilometre down the canyon and—'

'Lewis!' broke in May. 'Get back in here *now!*'

They were waiting, tight-lipped, in the common room. They had projected the short transcript onto a working area of the wall. Paul saw the pattern of interruptions the moment he entered.

Is this far enough. I hope so. Get on with it then. May. Can you hear me. We can hear you. Is Vandamme with you. Yes. Then listen to this. I think there is someone else with us out here. I don't know who or what they are but I know it's not one of us. It has to be someone ???????????????????? the evidence I have I think there is som?????????????? us out here. There's one

two three four of us and there must be ?????????????????? you get
that. Did you get it. We got it. Do you want us to try another
location. No. You can come back in. You're sure. We could go
a kilometre down the canyon and. Lewis. Get back in here
now.

'I'm scared, Lewis,' said May.

'Why?' said Lewis expressionlessly. 'Nothing's happened
to us in ten years.'

But his eyes were fixed on the transcript. His mouth
moved silently, as if he were repeating the words to himself.
He must have read them two or three times. Then, slowly,
he lowered himself into a seat.

'I didn't believe it,' he said quietly. 'I just didn't believe it.
My God – how long has this been going on?'

'All the time, maybe,' said Vandamme. 'We might have
known sooner if we hadn't lost Thorsten but . . .'

'But it's hard to believe all the same.'

'Some things are so big you just don't see them.'

'My God!'

'Coffee?' said Paul.

'Yes, please.'

He left them to their shock and made his way to the
kitchen. He took down the white cups and clipped them to
the tray. He made the coffee and poured it. When he

rejoined the others, May and Lewis were both on their feet. They were agitated. May was waving her hands.

'. . . It's got to be something Earth's doing!' she was saying. 'It's got to be! Hasn't it?'

'Earth is eight light-hours away, there and back,' Lewis answered. 'Anything that could react this quickly to signals from out here must be out here with us. Not just orbiting the planet. It's here on the moon with us.'

'But it must at least be *human*, mustn't it? To understand what we were saying?'

'It's hard to imagine what else it could be. But . . .'

'But?'

'But if it's a human then it's a pretty damned simple-minded one. What's it jamming? The words *someone else*. To a human that's as good as telling us there *is* someone else. If it's a human, then it's one that's got absolutely no under-standing of how other humans will perceive what it does.'

'Could it be the We?'

'Eight hours away,' Lewis repeated wearily. 'Plus its reaction time, which is going to be hours if not days. It's not the We, whatever it is.'

'Can I show you something?' said Vandamme quietly.

'Please.'

'Field readings: seventeen: zero four: twelve hundred,' said Vandamme to the wall.

The screen filled with figures.

'Those are pretty damned high,' said Lewis, eyeing them. 'Is that what was going on when we were out there?'

'They are extreme, Lewis. Although in fact they are slightly less extreme than the recordings we took during Paul's first excursion. And I think that if we repeated the experiment several times we would find both that the level of activity would fall and that the accuracy of the jamming would improve each time we did it.'

'Why?'

'Because that's how a brain learns,' said May. 'That's what you're saying, isn't it, Van? That's how a brain learns.'

'It's hiding in the shadows,' said Vandamme at last.

Lewis stirred. 'What's that?'

'Something Paul said to me. It's in the shadow. On the side of the planet away from the Sun. That's why Earth hasn't found it. It's hiding behind the planet.'

'You're saying it's the tail? The tail is *alive*?'

'It's responding. And it doesn't want to be found.'

'Found by whom?'

'By Earth. It knows Earth is there.'

'But – a field isn't *life*,' said Lewis. 'How can it be? Where's its DNA?'

'It doesn't need DNA. It needs a way of copying itself.

244

Life is a pattern that copies itself. That's all. Once it's reached a population of several thousand, then it's stable enough to survive in the long term. And to mutate and adapt.'

'Several thousand?' repeated May.

'I don't understand,' said Lewis. 'Are you saying it's one thing, or thousands?'

'Both, perhaps.'

A pattern, Paul thought. One that used energy, became complex and replicated itself. The action of the exterior sub-storms crowded on the interior ones and forced them to split into little copies of themselves, so that there were always more to replace those that perished on the edge of the tail.

How could it be intelligent? A magnetic source might excite particles so that they reacted like the impulses from a nerve cell. But how could these reactions become thought? How did they link and feed back to one another? How did it learn and remember? What stimuli or process of selection had cultivated it to reach its current state?

When, in its history, had it learned fear?

For it was afraid. After aeons of knowing only the planet, the solar wind and itself, it had felt a sudden change: an increase in radio communications sourced from one tiny rock planet circling closely around the star. A torrent of signals, growing and growing in intensity as mankind worked through the technological advances of radio, television, telephone and the World Ear. To a thing that perceived the radio spectrum, it must have been as dramatic as a second sun flaring at the heart of the solar system. A new light that drove the thing scurrying for darkness.

And then worse had come. More transmissions had begun, here, sourced from a fleck of rock that until now had been silent and meaningless as it orbited through the magnetic tail. The new star, Earth, had reached out and planted a seed of itself here, so that all space became full of its chatter and there was nowhere to hide. It must have felt like an invasion. Or a knife drawn across the skin.

But the field – if it was a field – was not defenceless. Bursts of particles could override anything in its immediate vicinity. To begin with it must have suppressed all the new transmissions indiscriminately, confounding the World Ear networks and bringing construction of the station to a temporary halt. But it was also capable of listening and of learning. It had been bathed in signals from Earth for more than a hundred years. It had come to know them, so that it could distinguish and jam only those transmissions that seemed to relate directly to itself – the periodic surveys of the tail, where the heart of its being lay, and a little lone voice on the ice which cried, *There must be someone else.*

*   *   *

'. . . But you're not making sense either!' Vandamme complained. 'Why can't it be an ST2 event?'

'Because there's never *been* one!' cried Lewis. 'We've been looking and looking for a hundred years, far beyond this solar system, and there has never been anything! Not a bleep, not even a microbe. Certainly nothing capable of learning – and learning our language!'

'It's something, though,' said Vandamme. 'Isn't it? Something that can only have been done by some level of intelligence?'

Lewis paused.

'Well . . .' But he did not go on.

'I think Earth suspects it,' Paul said.

'How do you know that?'

'I was thinking about this when I shut myself away – why I was sent here, when the station was already manned. The reason I had decided on did not work. You were right about that. But you were wrong that my work – our work – is not important. I was sent to investigate the corruptions. Not because Earth wanted the lost data but because they wanted to know about the corruptions themselves. They wanted me to repeat Thorsten's search, to eliminate for sure the possibility that the source was in the station. That alone mattered enough to get me sent out here. What interests Earth that much? ST2.'

'You think Earth *knows* it's here?'

Paul shook his head. 'No. Certainly no one person does. It would have been in my briefings. But collectively, yes, when all the different thoughts of all the different people come together – I think Earth is interested.'

'It's caught a scent,' brooded Lewis. 'It's seen a print in the sand, when it thought it was alone. What do we—?'

'Shouldn't we report?' said Vandamme.

Strange, thought Paul, how those few words affected them! Now that he was used to looking at faces, the details jumped to his eye. He saw Lewis and May, surprised, exchanging glances. He saw the slight stiffening of Lewis's cheeks, like a man in the presence of danger. Vandamme herself was tight-lipped and pale, as if she had felt a sudden pain even as she spoke. Her eyes were on the air ahead of her. Her hands came together in her lap, and when they clutched each other the knuckles went white.

'I wouldn't want to take the risk,' said Lewis slowly. 'If it thought this was a real ST2 event, the We would come here. It would expand the station, ship out however much shielding it needed, build an environment in which it could operate no matter what the cost. It's what it's been waiting for. More than anything.'

'It would take time,' said Paul.

'Years. But years don't matter. If it comes here, then

everything we're trying to do here would be finished.'

'But we don't have to submit,' said May.

'You're thinking of us as individuals. But our collective effort, our opportunity to hand it on to succeeding, un-contaminated generations, would be lost. Agree?'

'But – in scientific terms – what's the point of us being here if we don't report it?' said Vandamme. 'It's what we're here *for*.'

'It's what Earth sent us here for. But we are not Earth. We must decide what is right for us. Van – Earth is evil. You've said so yourself.'

'I know! I know! But – I don't know what I'm to do! Couldn't this be its salvation?'

'The We isn't a human. It isn't a scientist either,' said Lewis. 'It's a feral child that's grown by itself in the locked room of space. It's had no relationships, nothing to teach it how to respond to another being. What do you think it will do if it finds that there's something else in the room with it?'

'Study it!'

'That's the scientist's answer. But there's more than one way of studying a thing. Haven't you ever seen a child study a fly by pulling off its wings? How did the European explorers *study* the peoples they found in Africa and the Americas? By enslavement, exploitation and conquest! If this

249

thing is hiding itself from Earth, then it's wise – very wise. Its only hope is to escape notice, isn't it? And that we – the four of us – will help it to do so.'

'I need to pray.'

'But we can't pray with you, Van. And this is something we must decide together.'

Vandamme was silent.

'Whatever we decide, Van, it will be your task to study it,' said Lewis gently. '*We* still need to know about it, don't we? We'll need to know everything that you and Paul can find out . . . Paul, are you going to vote?'

Paul stirred. 'Vote?'

'Consensual decision-making. We each say what we think. If the majority of us say that we should not report to Earth, then all of us, even those who disagree, agree to be bound by that decision. It's the key to any free society. And that's what we are. The more I think about this . . . This is a fundamental moment – literally fundamental, because we're laying our foundations. Up to now we've only been hiding. Now we have a choice – to do as Earth wills us to do, or to take another course. Do you see? This is where we start to make our own future. Will you?'

Paul hesitated. Years of training yelped at him. But Lewis . . .

Lewis and May, and Erin Vandamme . . .

These were the most important people in his life now. There was no one else.

'Yes,' he said. 'If you will have me back.'

'You've never left us, Paul. But we need you to follow the rules. What's your vote?'

'I will agree with you,' Paul said.

'Which in this case means you agree that we should not inform Earth. Do you understand that?'

'Yes.'

'Good. So that is clear then . . .'

'I'm going to pray,' said Vandamme. She rose to her feet and loped down the long room towards the airlock.

'Van!' said May. 'Don't be upset . . .' She and Lewis exchanged glances. She got to her feet and hurried after Vandamme, but Vandamme had reached the airlock and closed the seal before she got there. May pursued her into the airlock, calling, 'Van! Van!' as she went.

'Where did that come from?' said Lewis softly. 'Where the *hell* did that come from? Report to Earth? She hates the place more than any of us. Or I thought she did.'

'Maybe she does not know what she thinks,' said Paul.

'You think it's that? Science says one thing, belief says another? But she talks of salvation! Salvation – just because there's someone else?' Lewis shook his head. 'I don't get it. I just can't tell which direction she's coming from these days . . .'

He was staring at the airlock through which the women had disappeared, as if wishing his eyes could bore through it, through the wall of the chambers beyond and into the skull of Erin Vandamme.

'It may be because of you, Paul. In a way. She's been all frozen up for years – like a bit of our landscape, round at the poles where it's dark for ages at a time. And when at last the Sun gets round there, the crust stirs right up – flows, geysers, icy volcanism, the lot. So maybe it's a hopeful sign. But for the time being – just to be on the safe side – can you lock her out of the communications system?'

'Lock her out?'

'Remove her permissions to use the laser and the radio. I don't want her suddenly deciding she's got to signal Earth behind our backs.'

'She won't do that.'

'You can't be sure what she'll do.'

'No,' Paul admitted. He thought there was something terrible about removing someone's ability to communicate.

'All right,' said Lewis at last. 'If you don't want to do it, I will. But tell me something else. Is there a way of sending a radio signal that will *not* be picked up by Earth?'

'A signal?'

'I want to use the radio but I don't want Earth to hear.'

Paul thought. 'Yes. We wait until we are in the shadow again. Then we send a signal to a crawler. The satellite will fire at once, at the surface, and the planet will block any rebound.'

'It'll be days before we're back in the shadow! Isn't there another way?'

'Not so certain.'

'All right,' he said. 'All right. It's probably best.' He looked thoughtful for a moment. 'I'm glad we've got you back, Paul. I'm really, really glad. For the first time in years I feel what we're trying to do may actually be possible.'

'What *are* you trying to do?'

'Well, first – we're going to talk to the thing.'

XVIII

Their message read: *Do not be afraid. We know you are here.*

Paul had it displayed on the working area of the wall in the main common room. It was the best place for everyone to see what was going on. He had set the ceiling view to show the sky above the station, with the planet once again a thin crescent and the distant Sun poised above it. Lewis hovered, unable to keep still.

'It's like the angel's message,' he said. '*Do not be afraid.*'

'It is a good way to start,' said Paul.

'Van would want us to add *Good News of Great Joy.*'

He was trying to get May to smile. She was sitting moodily against the wall. Her skin was pale and her eye-sockets dark. She had told them she had slept badly. Now she pulled a face.

'You're assuming that we're the angels,' she said.

'Do you want me to add it—?' Paul began.

'No! God, no!' Lewis snorted. 'That would just confuse it. How much longer?'

'We're still in the penumbra,' said Paul, for the third time in half an hour. He wished that Lewis would stop bouncing up and down behind his back.

'Yes, but how much *longer*?'

'Ten minutes, to be sure.'

'God! I'm going to burst, I think. A mind as big as that! And in a moment we're going to be talking to it! Can you imagine what it must know?' Lewis turned and took a big skip, pushing far harder than he needed in his impatience, so that he sailed past Paul to the end of the chamber and had to put out a hand to stop himself from colliding with the airlock. He faced them.

'Seriously, about the future,' he said. 'I've been thinking how following generations might sustain themselves and so on . . .'

Following generations, Paul thought. Not just one but many. It was not the first time Lewis had said it, either. He was back to assuming that they – the four of them – would produce children and grandchildren, a population with enough genetic diversity to last, triumphantly, where all Earth had failed.

He was assuming something enormous between Paul and Erin Vandamme.

And Paul looked at it, in the secrecy of his mind, while his eyes stared unseeing at the screen. He thought of the quiet woman in the chamber beyond the airlock. He remembered the feel of her arms around him and the sound of her voice saying, '*Paul.*'

He did not know the answer.

'. . . We go down,' Lewis said. 'We say goodbye to the surface and we dig. The further down we go, the warmer it will get. Pressure will increase too. That would make a big difference to the engineering. How about that?'

'If we want more pressure we must dig a long way,' said Paul. 'How far down do you want to go?'

'It depends on how quickly the temperature rises. And also on what the construction crawlers can do. But maybe – about two hundred kilometres.'

'Two *hundred*!'

'Around that point you get to the liquid mantle, trapped between the ice sheets. There will be currents down there, and we can tap those for energy . . .

'Eden in a tunnel of ice,' he added. 'How do you like that?'

'How do we insulate the tunnels?' said Paul.

'I've some ideas about that . . .'

'You've been thinking about this.'

'I've been *thinking* about it for ten years, Paul. But now, please God, I've actually got a reason to start doing something about it.'

'How many will we be?' asked May.

Good question, thought Paul.

'Time will tell,' said Lewis smoothly. 'Speaking of time, Paul . . . ?'

'Another few minutes.'

'God! Can't we just send it?'

'Should we ask Van to do the sending?' said Paul. 'ST2 is her field.'

'She won't come,' said May. 'I looked in there a while ago. She's still just sitting there, staring at the wall.'

'She'll get over it,' said Lewis.

Paul wondered what it was that had taken May down to Vandamme's room after her sleepless night.

Whatever it was, she hadn't found it there.

'It was blocking her communications that did it,' May said. 'Her science has nowhere to go. You've taken it away from her.'

'It can't be helped,' said Lewis.

There was a short silence.

'We must have sunlight,' Paul said. 'For the plants.'

'They can stay on the surface. We process them remotely and have the product transported down to us. It's maintaining the living quarters in this environment that's the big burden. But down there, with more pressure and a much higher temperature, we could sustain a population of – well, God knows how many. Time, Paul?'

'. . . Yes.'

'Then send it, please.'

Paul reached for the control. *Click.* The message disappeared.

Together they stared at the blank screen.

'How will it answer, do you think?'

'If it can understand our signals . . .'

'That doesn't mean it can communicate with them.'

They went on looking at the screen.

'Of course,' said Lewis, 'it won't be an entirely un-contaminated mind. It's been picking up noise from Earth for a hundred years. How much of its thinking has it learned from us?'

'Do you think it will be able to help us . . . you know, survive?'

'Not directly. But there's no telling what we might learn. Maybe the field itself could be a source of—'

'What's that?'

A familiar red rectangle flashed in the bottom right corner of the screen.

'Just an alert. It can wait.'

'What do you suppose its reaction time is?'

'We know that. Seconds, at most, when it was jamming the crawler. Anticipation made it faster still.'

'It's being a lot slower this time. Does it know we're talking to it?'

'Check the field readings?' said Lewis.

Paul called them up. They danced in jiggling yellow lines against the darkness of the canyon wall on the display.

'High!' said Lewis. 'But we're well into the tail, of course. How high were they before we sent the message?'

Paul called up the readings of five minutes earlier and superimposed them on the wall.

'They've jumped, haven't they?'

'They have.'

'We've given it something to think about, anyway . . . My God!'

A huge spike in the readings had flickered briefly up the wall, there and gone like a lightning flash in the storms of Earth.

'I hope it doesn't do that too often. I'm not sure—'

Something beeped. In the bottom right of the working area another alert was flashing red. There were letters. Paul did not recognize the acronym.

'Damn!' said Lewis. 'Why's that happening? I'll have to sort that. Paul, for God's sake tell it not to shout!'

Paul flicked to the message screen. Nothing was showing,

except for the red alert lights flashing in the corner. *Three lights now.*

'It is not making sense,' he said.

'Tell it not to shout.'

Paul picked out a message. *That is too much. Be more gentle.* 'Will that do?'

'Who knows?' said May.

'Will that do, Lewis?'

'He's gone to sort out those alerts,' said May. 'It must be the strength of the thing's signal that's doing it. It's like a magnetic storm, interfering with some of our systems. Look – it's dying off now. Try sending.'

Paul sent the message. Over the microphone he could hear Lewis muttering in his chamber. Lewis must have opened the channel so that he could listen to what was going on in the common room.

'Ah!' said May. One of the red lights had gone off.

Then it came back again. So did two more.

'Lewis!' called May.

'I know, damn it!' came Lewis's voice. 'What's it doing?'

'There is no message,' said Paul. Then he said, 'Field readings, current.' The screen changed.

'Oh my God!'

'What's it doing?' snapped Lewis. 'What the hell's it . . . ?'

He must have called up the field readings himself then, for his voice died away.

'It hasn't understood,' said May.

'What's it saying, Paul?' called Lewis. 'Any idea?'

'I don't think it's *saying* anything. It's just— Shit! Look at that!'

A string of error messages started to mount the screen.

'Particle readings, current,' said Paul. The screen changed obediently. Still the error messages mounted.

'Lewis . . .' said May.

She was looking at the particle readings, trying to control her voice.

'Yes,' said Lewis. 'I see it.'

'Is that what's damaging the systems?'

'Shouldn't be . . . Maybe . . .'

There was a short silence. Then Lewis said, 'If the computers are susceptible . . . I can't predict what will happen to the life-support functions.'

May and Paul looked at each other.

The computing systems governed everything in the station – including the heating and life-support systems. The computing systems were distributed in the outer layers, to exploit the conductivity that could be achieved at low temperatures. The outer layers were most exposed to the magnetic storm. The computers had a five hundred per cent redundancy, in case of damage. But a storm like this might affect all the systems at once.

'I'm increasing the density in the outer layers,' said Lewis. 'I'm going to take it as high as I can, to give us maximum protection. That means the heat loss from the station will increase. It's going to get chilly.'

There was a short silence.

'When you say *chilly* . . .' May began.

'How low will it get? I don't know . . .

'We should get into suits,' he added. 'Just in case. Suits, both of you. Keep your helmets to hand. I'll tell you if you have to put them on.'

'You had better get Van,' muttered May.

Paul yielded his seat to her. He skipped down the common room and through the airlock. He called at Vandamme's seal. There was no answer. He entered. Vandamme was sitting in the middle of her chamber, surrounded by the images of ice on her walls.

'You have to come,' Paul said.

Vandamme did not answer. Only the blink of her eyes as she stared at the walls told Paul that she was still living and had not somehow taken her own life in her despair.

'You have to come,' Paul told her. He reached and shook her by the shoulder.

Vandamme tensed. She glared, not at Paul but at a point on the distant moonscape. 'Why?' she said.

'We're being attacked.'

It came in waves, again and again – lines of force coinciding over the station, bringing highly energetic particles down from space. Paul felt his stomach lurch each time he saw the numbers spike on the screen. He thought of the radiation pouring out of the sky. He thought of the particles smashing into the gas molecules in the outer layers, showering into thousands more particles, bombarding, showering again . . . They could not penetrate far into the station, but to reach the computer units they would not have to. And those impacts would have other effects – X-rays and gamma rays. Nothing in the station would stop gamma – not gas, not chamber wall, not pressure suit or human skin. If the designers on Earth had seen radiation as a serious hazard they would have buried the station in the ice. They hadn't. And now the creature was trying to kill them with it, just as health workers on Earth would kill a cancerous cell.

Cold was creeping through the air. Paul felt it like a bar of ice pressing on his forehead. His breath frosted when he exhaled. He desperately wanted to put his helmet on, power his suit and sit in warmth and complete protection. But the power in the suits would only last so long. There was no use exhausting it now if they were going to need it later. He sat and watched and shivered.

Vandamme was in the common room with him. They sat together on the inflated seating, with their eyes and noses peeping over the tops of their high collars and their frosty breath fuming upwards like the steam from little volcanoes. Their hands, muffled in their great gauntlets, were too clumsy for the workstation controls. They watched the screen and controlled it by voice. Behind them the seal to Lewis's chamber was open. Lewis was in there with his legs in his suit and the top half of it spilling over his knees like a clumsy blanket, so that his hands were free and he could use every possible resource that his workstation gave him. Paul had looked in to see him there, muttering over the controls, squinting at the screen while May watched over his shoulder and the brightly coloured images of long-ago Earth still changed and changed upon his walls.

Another wave. It did not seem angry or fearful. It was like the action of a huge tongue, probing and probing at something that irritated in the mouth. Each time the system registered a new peak Paul wondered how much higher it could go.

Not even the World Ear could have given him an answer to that.

More error messages appeared. Malfunction reports from

one of the computer sites, from an auxiliary transmitter, from a search crawler. Particle damage in all cases. All had had shielding. All had been overwhelmed. The loss of the computer site might be trivial, or it might be serious. Everything depended on what the effects were and how Lewis could compensate for them. It depended too on what happened next: where the next chink in the station's armour would be.

They could do nothing but wait.

Paul turned to the woman beside him.

'Erin?' he said.

Her face – as much as Paul could see of it – did not change at all. It was as if she did not think Paul could have been speaking to her.

'Erin. That's your name, isn't it?'

'Yes,' she said at last.

'Do you mind if I call you that?'

She seemed to think about it. 'No, I don't mind,' she said.

'Helmets,' said Lewis's voice.

Fumble. Heave the huge thing over his head and lower it onto the rigid collar. Click. Twist. Power the suit. Check the displays. *Ex: 1.0 Suit: 1.0 Temp: -1°*. (Only minus one? Surely it had been lower than that!) And reach over, already feeling the warmth beginning to build around his legs, and check her fitting, and wait while she checked his.

'Lewis?' said Paul. 'We have our helmets on.'

'Good.'

'Are you suiting up too now?'

'Not yet. Not until I really have to. But, Paul?'

'Yes?'

'You have to carry on trying to get through to it. Wait until the wave has died and then de-helmet and do it by voice. I think it's dying now. Can you see what you can do?'

Paul looked at the record of messages he had sent each time the waves had died. *We cannot understand you . . . Your signal is too strong . . . You are hurting us . . . You are damaging us – be more gentle . . . You must use words that we use . . .*

'What do you want me to say this time?'

'As before. Tell it that we don't understand and that it's hurting us. Get it to calm down.'

'No,' said Erin Vandamme. 'Don't transmit.'

'Why the hell not?' cried Lewis. 'We've *got* to get through to it!'

'We *are* getting through to it! That's how it knows where we are.'

There was silence.

'It doesn't sense the station,' she said. 'It can't see and it can't touch. It senses the transmissions. It reacts to them.'

'Why should it stop hitting us just because we stop transmitting?'

'When pain goes, you stop rubbing at it, don't you?' said May.

'The moon's orbit will carry us away from where it last sensed us,' said Erin.

'And out of the tail,' said Paul.

'They're right, Lewis,' said May. 'Maybe we should give up for the time being.'

'But we've got to talk to the thing!'

'We can try again any time. Right now we're putting the station in danger. And ourselves.'

'What's going to be different— Damn!'

More alerts were scrolling up the screen – a long string of them.

'That's one of the algae tanks.'

'It's all right,' said Lewis. 'I knew that would happen.'

'Won't we lose the harvest?'

'Not so long as— Hell! What's *that*?'

Another alert. Once again the acronym meant nothing to Paul. He heard Lewis muttering to himself.

'Lewis?' said May. 'What do you think?'

'Yes, all right. Paul – no transmission please. Of any sort. Shut down anything you think might be emitting. And don't use the intercom unless you have to. We'll sit this passage out and then take stock.'

'Will you suit up now, Lewis?' said Paul.

'I said no transmission, please.'

They sat in silence, watching the numbers dance on the screen and the relentless march of the error alerts super-imposed upon them. One was from the second auxiliary transmitter again. A number were from the Knowledge Store, which appeared to be responding to a query no one had sent. Most of the others Paul did not recognize. They were things that only Lewis knew about.

Paul thought about the shielding engineers – the people back on Earth who had been given the task of estimating how much magnetic interference and radiation the systems would be exposed to and of designing equipment to tolerate the load. There would have been good minds among them, lifetimes spent in the study of particle physics, modelling programs and the properties of materials. They had had the experience of a hundred years of space exploration to draw upon. What would they have felt if they were here now? If they were ranged behind him, watching the screen with him as the numbers danced and the errors mounted? Guilt, that the magnetic field was more intense than they had allowed for? Or pride, that so far only a small proportion of the station systems had actually failed?

Or would they feel nothing at all? Would it be a fatalistic shrug of the shoulders? *It wasn't our fault. Department X provided the readings. Department Y predicted the maximum strength of the field. We did what we were asked to do. And then Department Z insisted ...* It wasn't just the shielding engineers that the crew must rely on. It was everyone – everyone who had been a part of the great network, the mini-We that had designed, built, transported and erected the station out here. And he was depending too on the great We itself, which must have imposed the resource limits that the project had worked to. One failure, one honest miscalculation that escaped detection, could mean that the whole station failed now. That he, Paul Munro, would fail with it.

And that had been true ever since he had been laid inside his transport capsule back in the warm air of Earth.

A touch woke him from his thoughts. Erin Vandamme had tapped him on the shoulder. She mimed removing her helmet.

He checked the display. *Ex: 0.9 Suit: 1.0 Temp: -6°.* Pressure in the living quarters had fallen. The cold had deepened. It was all perfectly survivable, for the moment. But things were happening that were never meant to happen. And it might suddenly get worse.

Still she was miming at him. He hesitated. Then he nodded and gently powered down his suit. He felt it sag onto his body. He felt his ears pop and the sudden increase of cold. He lifted his hands to his helmet. It came free just as Erin removed hers. They looked at each other over their high collars.

'Why did you ask me that?' she said.

'What?'

'About my name.'

'You called me Paul, didn't you?'

She hesitated. Then she said, 'It's not because you own me now?'

'*Own* you?'

'Because of what I did.'

He looked blankly at her. She looked away.

'I've been wondering,' she said. 'I think about you so much. Why you are really here. Why you say the things you do. You always seem to have reasons. I look at each thing you do and say, and I think, Yes, this is why . . . But that doesn't tell me why I've felt so afraid of you . . .'

'You are afraid of me?' he said, bewildered.

'Sometimes . . . Sometimes, yes I am. And yet when you come through my door I want you to stay and talk to me. When you stay in your chamber I want to go in to you . . .'

'What makes you afraid of me?'

She laughed – a nervous little laugh. She put her head in her hands. 'Is it going to be meaningless to you? Or are you being very clever? I don't know. I've no way of knowing . . . Do you know what Lewis calls this place sometimes? He calls it "Eden". You've heard him say that, haven't you?'

'Yes.'

'He likes the name because that was the place in the story where the first man and woman met – the father and mother of all men. He wants a new race of men in this place, of course . . .

'What he's forgotten is that the man and woman were not alone in Eden. There was – someone else – there with them. The Serpent. That's who I'm afraid of.'

'Serpent?'

Paul blinked slowly. Nothing came. Groaning aloud, he reached for the keyboard.

'How do you spell it?' he asked.

She told him. He called up the Knowledge Store. The entry he found was one she herself had written. He read it. It was the story she was talking to him about.

'What did you do?' he asked.

'About what?'

'You did something that made you think I owned you. What was it?'

'I told May what you said. You remember – about her child being alone here after we had all gone. Of course she's been telling herself it won't be and of course she fears it will. It hit her when I said it. Very hard. I meant it to.'

'I heard, I think. Lewis said you were not kind.'

'Kind! I wanted to punish her. I *knew* that was what I was doing. And I was so pleased with myself for resisting you! And I fell at once. She's been miserable ever since. You must have noticed.'

Paul nodded. He had noticed. Today he had, when they had been preparing the message.

He dismissed the entry from his screen.

'I am not that,' he said.

'What are you, then?'

'Maybe I am Change. Change can make you afraid too.'

She seemed to think about that.

'I should tell her I'm sorry,' she said. 'But I can't. It just sticks in me. I can't!'

After a moment Paul put his hand on hers. Through the thickness of their two suit gauntlets he could just feel the shapes of fingers, remote but there, alive within the protective layers. He thought she might take her hand away, but she did not. Neither of them spoke.

It was cold. He was shivering in his suit and his face felt numb. He thought that they should both put their helmets back on. But he did not want to take his hand from hers. Just at the moment the levels on the screen seemed to be falling, anyway. That was another alert cancelled. Well done, Lewis. How long would this go on?

'Do you remember Earth?' said Erin.

'Yes, of course.'

'No, but really remember it? Can you remember the dampness and coolness of the air in the early morning? I can't. I know it was like that but I can't remember what it felt like.' She sighed. 'I was looking at a picture of clouds, a couple of watches back. I'd forgotten the way their undersides looked when it was about to rain – all dark and feathery, and those dark streaks below them slanting towards the ground.'

'Yes, I remember,' he said.

'Sometimes I dream of it,' he added.

'It's a strange thing to worry about,' she said. 'If this is the last hour of my life, I should be asking for forgiveness – from May, from you, from everybody. But that's what I really feel. Some little cell in me containing that memory has died, and I can't bring it back. That's what—'

'I don't think it is.'

'What?'

'The last hour of your life.'

'I'm glad you're so sure.'

He pointed to the screen. The wave of activity was still falling. The alerts had stopped.

XIX

'I can find no pattern in the waves,' said Paul. 'Nor can Hunter. It was not trying to communicate.'

They were in the common room again, bathed in the warm cream light of the walls. The temperature was normal. The unnerving cold was gone. The damage checks had been carried out, the results analysed, repair tasks prioritized. In the sky above them the crescent of the planet would be swelling again as the moon swung away from the tail.

But the signs of the last hours were written on their faces. No one had slept. No one – not even Erin – had gone off to shut themselves in their room. They had clustered together in the common room as if for comfort, taking turns to work on the main screen, making each other coffee and bringing in food at odd times. The schedule of watches, set mealtimes and rest periods was ignored and no one mentioned that they were ignoring it. It was as if that too had been shattered by some stray particle back in the passage of the tail.

'Maybe it can't communicate,' said Lewis. 'Maybe its

intelligence is enough to recognize words but not to use them. Like a dog's, say.'

'A very big dog,' said Erin. 'And wild. You still want to talk with it?'

'If I can.'

'Why? You want it to sit up and beg?'

Lewis threw up his hands. 'Because it's intelligent! Because we're sharing its space. Because it knows things we don't, maybe. We should treat it like a person, with respect!'

'It *attacked* us. And this station wasn't designed for high levels of radiation.'

'High?' said Lewis. 'I mean, yes, it was more than advisable, certainly. And over a sustained period—'

'Lewis,' said Paul. 'We shouldn't be risking *any* more exposure than we must. May should not at all.'

May said nothing. She was sitting with her knees tight together and her elbows held close against her sides. She was looking down at her hands, which were tucked in between her thighs. A pink spot had appeared upon her cheeks, just as it had when Lewis had handed around Earth's response to Paul's message about her child. She was angry because she was helpless. She had written about cradling her child, even as particles fell from space. But the womb could not protect the embryo from electrons moving with the energy imparted by thousands of volts. If that were repeated and repeated, every six days, some price would have to be paid. She knew that. The embryo was the most vulnerable of them all.

'All right,' said Lewis, frowning. 'There is that. So what do you think we should do?'

'We should shut down all transmissions,' said Erin. 'We send nothing to anything by radio. Not to crawlers, not to Earth, not to each other. Let it think it's killed us.'

'For how long?'

'Indefinitely.'

Lewis raised his eyebrows. 'Total radio shutdown? That's impractical. We have to control the utilities somehow.'

'We use it as little as possible, then. We suspend all search operations – why should I go on searching if we know we're not going to report what I find? We suspend the active experiments too. And we only use the utility crawlers when we absolutely have to. We communicate with Earth only by laser. In the meantime we try to map how the field works – what's keeping it stable. We interfere with it as little as possible, at least to begin with. In time maybe we can try stimulating it again. But I'd want to be very gradual, both for its sake and ours.'

'Earth will complain,' said May.

Lewis shrugged. 'I'm not worried about Earth. We'll tell them the transmitters were damaged in a magnetic storm. It's pretty well true. If it's a question of our survival—'

'I am worried about Earth,' said Paul.

'What do you mean?'

They were looking at him – all three of them. Lewis was frowning a little, as if the very mention of Earth was enough to cause suspicion. May had a lock of her long hair caught in the corner of her mouth. And Erin – her eyes were widening as she turned to him on the seat beside her. Somehow she knew what was coming from his mouth.

'Erin was right,' he said. 'We must think again. We must report what we have found.'

'We've taken that vote, Paul,' said Lewis, with a dangerous softness.

'We must take it again.'

'*Why?* For what *possible* reason? Earth is eight years' travel away! Even if we called it now and confessed everything it would make no difference! We would still have to find a way of living with this thing. There's nothing Earth can do to help us and everything it can do to destroy us and the way we think!'

'No. Not for help. I know that . . .'

He leaned forward because Lewis was leaning forward. He looked into Lewis's red face.

'I thought about this during the attack. About the people who made this place and how we depend on what they did.

Lewis, you want to cut us off from Earth. To do that you must make everyone who will ever live here think Earth is evil. You will raise your children and say to them Earth is evil, evil, evil! Earth is not evil. Things have changed, yes. But things are always changing. Look at Hunter and see how far we've come! Now the "I" is weaker and the "We" is stronger. Is that evil? And Lewis – you said the We was a feral child, because for it there was no one else. If you cut us off from Earth, we will be the same. We will need someone else in the universe. We always have done.'

'How can you say that?' cried Lewis. 'They've no moral choice any more. They're slaves! And if it comes here, we'll be slaves too!'

'Lewis . . . When I woke and found I was without my World Ear, I wept. Didn't you?'

'And that was done to you, and you were sent out here. You call that *human*?'

'I suppose – yes,' said Paul. 'Just now you said "moral choice". I know what you mean. It's rules for living with others . . .'

'It's more than that,' said Erin.

'I've lived on Earth, and with you, and I've been alone. There are rules on Earth. They are different from what we have here – very different. But they are still rules, even if everyone follows them without thinking. Only when you are alone are there no rules.' He grinned sourly. 'I know that now.'

'I see,' said Lewis, watching him. 'But you agree we have rules here too. Do you mean that if we vote again, you will be bound by whatever we decide?'

Paul hesitated.

'Yes,' he said.

'And if we cannot agree – if it's two against two – then we must do nothing. Because doing nothing keeps the option open but sending the message is irrevocable?'

'Yes,' said Paul slowly.

'I agree with Paul,' said Erin.

'I thought you would,' said Lewis irritably. 'But May and I—'

'Paul's right,' said May.

There was a moment's silence.

'Don't *look* at me like that!' she snapped. 'He's right. We need more people out here. Set any rules you like for them. Tell them that no one lands with a working World Ear – anything. But they've got to come.'

'We can't stop them importing the World Ear,' said Lewis firmly. 'The first ones might respect the rule but it would quickly get too important—'

'Then I don't care. We need more people here.'

'There will be, May! Before any ship can get out here—'

'What – from just the four of us? Two of us, even?'

'It's the only safe way—'

'*Safe?*' May's voice rose. 'How old is Van now? How long are you going to wait for her to come out of herself? Can she have a child? What'll happen to it? Will she survive? Will I? What if they're the same sex? Will we have to try again?'

'Leave me out of this!' snapped Erin. 'Leave me *and* Paul out of this.'

'We *can't* leave you out of this, Van!' said Lewis – and at the same time May cried, 'I *am* leaving them out! And even if I don't . . . You heard what she said. It needs thousands!'

'That's in the long term,' said Lewis. 'This is just a population bottleneck. Humans have had them before—'

'This won't work!'

'You don't know that!' cried Lewis.

'I don't need to *know* it! I can look at the chances, can't I? *I don't want my kid to die alone!*'

'Look, we've had a scare,' said Lewis. 'Our confidence has been shaken. This is the wrong time—'

'I want to take the vote now,' said May. 'Paul – you said we should contact Earth?'

Paul drew breath. He let it go again. 'Yes,' he said.

'Van?'

'Yes,' said Erin. 'On that one point, yes.'

'And so do I,' said May. She faced Lewis.

'That's it, then,' she said. 'That's what we'll do.'

She skipped away across the common room.

'May!' Lewis cried. She did not look back. '*May!*'

She reached the door to her chamber. She opened it. When the seal hissed shut behind her they were left in silence. Lewis's face was dark. His eyes turned to Paul. Paul shook his head, just slightly. He would not lock anyone out of the communications. Nor would he let Lewis do so – not this time.

For a moment the two men looked at each other. Then Lewis took three long steps down to the other end of the common room. He came to the airlock seal and passed through it. He closed it behind him. Paul let out his breath. No one said anything.

It was five minutes before Paul wondered why Lewis had gone into the outer layers.

By then the pressure in the airlock was already falling.

XX

Now he was in the airlock himself. He was checking the seals on the back of May's pressure suit. In a moment he would turn and let her check his. Then they would put the helmets on.

'Where is he?' asked May.

'In the main hangar,' came Erin's voice over the intercom. She was still in the living quarters, following Lewis's movements on the screen. 'Lewis, can you hear me?'

There was no answer.

Paul tapped May on the shoulder. She turned. He turned too, presenting his back to her. He felt her fingers tugging at the seals. This couldn't be hurried. If just one of them had failed to close properly, the suit would not power.

Come on, he thought. Come on!

All the time, he's getting further away.

What's he going to do?

'You knew what it meant to him!' Erin exploded.

'Shut up, Van,' said May.

'It's his *life*! This place and what it could be. You knew that. And you—'

'You agreed with me, didn't you? Just shut up!'

'He's your partner!'

He felt May tap his shoulder. He lunged for the helmet, lifted it, closed it on his collar. He powered the suit. The display flickered into life before his eyes. Through his earpiece he heard Erin mutter, 'We're going down. I know it.'

'Ready, Paul?' came May's voice.

'Ready,' he said.

'Van, we're ready. We're depressurizing the airlock now.'

'I can't see him,' said Erin.

There was a pause. 'We'll go to the hangar anyway,' said May. 'If you spot him—'

'Wait!'

There was something urgent in her voice.

'Oh my God!' she cried. 'You bitch! *You stupid bitch!*'

'What's *happening*? For God's sake, Van—'

'He's taken the red crawler. He's taking it – out.'

'*I'll* go after him!' Paul said. 'I'll suit up and ride on a crawler! One of you will have to pilot it.' And take the chance with the radio transmissions. They would have to. They were taking chances anyway, even now.

'Lewis,' Erin was saying. 'Please answer us! What are you doing?'

'We can't do that,' said May's voice.

'As long as I catch him quickly, it should be all right,' Paul said. 'When I came down in the red crawler we depressurized the cabin and—'

'You would fall off,' said May. 'The crawlers rock as they go. You would fall. And if you were hurt, we couldn't reach you. Not without the red crawler.'

'Hello, Lewis? Please answer!'

'You can't take the risk,' said May.

'Then we *have* to stop him leaving the station!'

'I can't!' cried Erin desperately. 'I need the override codes and only Lewis has those! We'd have to signal Earth—'

'Won't he just bore, like you did?' said May.

Paul called up the airlock controls and set them spinning. 'Power a crawler!' he snarled. 'I'm going after him.'

'Paul, don't be *stupid* . . .'

'He can keep you out,' said May.

'What?'

'Even if you reach the crawler he can keep you out. He keeps the inner door to the airlock open and the cabin pressurized. Then the outer door won't respond to anything, because of the fail-safe. He could just keep you hanging about out there. Until . . .'

284

Paul clenched his fists. Helpless, he sat down.

'He's out,' said Erin in a small, dry voice.

The suited figure of May seemed to wilt a little before Paul's eyes.

'You'd better come back in,' Erin said. 'He's out of the station. There's nothing you can do.'

'He'll be back,' said May, after a moment. 'If he had been going to . . .'

If he had been going to kill himself, thought Paul, he would have done – what?

Just opened his helmet in the outer layers?

Lewis was the station manager. If he did not come back . . .

There would be instructions in the Knowledge Store. Problems could be sent to Earth for diagnosis. But . . .

But they would have lost a lifetime's worth of experience of the most vital role in the station. Lewis had been here for ten years, managing tools and interactions that never worked quite as they should. He knew instinctively why condensation in the living quarters might be climbing too high. He knew what mix of feeds brought the best protein levels out of the lichens. He had steered them through the magnetic storm, as systems failed at random. Without him, they would suffer. They might make mistakes. Mistakes would be fatal.

What if they were attacked again?

The airlock had reached the pressure of the next layer. Paul looked at the readings on his display for a moment. He thought how useless it all was. Then, wearily, he sent it spinning back again.

'Lewis,' pleaded Erin. 'Can you hear us?'

Silence.

XXI

Once again they gathered around the console in the main living-quarter common room.

The screen relayed the view from the manned crawler. It showed the cairn and the pylon that marked where Thorsten lay. The cairn had been rebuilt. The remains of the dead man were hidden. Someone must have used a remotely controlled crawler to repair the little monument while Paul had been shut away in his chamber. Now it was almost as it had been when he had first seen it, except that the freshly piled lumps and canisters were no longer covered in frosted ammonia.

'You try,' said Erin. 'He just won't answer me.'

May shook her head. 'It's me he's mad at,' she said.

She looked at Paul.

Paul looked at the screen.

Nothing moved. The crawler was stationary. Its arms were not busy. Lewis was not doing anything. He was just sitting there, silent at the grave of his dead colleague.

Or was he? Was he? The crawler might be still, but . . .

'Subsystem menus,' said Paul.

And, 'Manned crawler.'

He wanted to know if the crawler airlock was still pressurized. If it was, then Lewis was still inside. If it was not, then he must have gone out. And if he had gone out . . .

He could not find what he needed. The crawler transmitted its display but not its internal readings. The Manual Override was locked. He could not take control. Still he hunted, knowing it was futile. And in his mind he battled with the thought: what if they did lose him?

'Field readings,' he said.

They were low, as they should be on this part of the orbit. They were just as they had been when he had first seen them, during his instruction with Vandamme on the use of the communications systems.

He opened the channel to the crawler again.

'Lewis? Lewis, this is Paul.'

A million-year-old instinct made him keep his voice low.

'Lewis – what's your power reading?'

Silence. And nothing changed in the pattern of the field. Could the thing hear him?

Could Lewis?

Was he still there? Was he already lying in a frozen heap by the crawler wheel? There was no answer. But if there was no movement soon, if that crawler did not turn and start back down the slope, then he would be dead. The auxiliary power pack did not last long. How long? It depended what the crawler was doing. At the moment it seemed to be doing nothing.

There was nothing he could do. Around him, the walls were bright cream, filling the room with soft light. But the ceiling was dark. In the centre of the display was the view of the gas giant hanging in space, as it had for billions of years and would for billions more. It was nearly three-quarters full. On its surface was a dark circular shape, a storm system many thousands of kilometres across – large enough to have swallowed the whole of the moon if it had fallen at that moment into the planet's surface. And now it looked exactly like an eye, peering down upon them.

The light was growing across the disc. He could actually see it move over the face of the planet as the moon swung further and further round to the Sun side. Up there, behind the planet – both behind him and ahead of him on the path of this orbit – was that other presence, silent, invisible, listening to his tiny voice as it squeaked unanswered on the surface of the frozen moon. Did it understand what was happening here? Probably not. Not yet. But it would be listening now. If there was anything in his words that troubled it, there might be another attack. It would be listening to everything that passed between him and the crawler.

If anything did pass. If they had not already said their last words.

He glanced at May. She saw his appeal but shook her head. She could not help. She could not reach Lewis now. It would make it worse if she tried.

He looked at Erin. Her eyes were hollow. Nine years ago she had spoken to a man who was outside the living quarters, and he had said, '*Goodbye, Erin.*' And now it was happening again. Her prayers, her isolation – it had all changed nothing. Out here everything was the same. Another man was about to die.

'Right,' said Lewis's voice, so suddenly that Paul jumped. 'Are you listening?'

'Yes,' said Paul.

'You can decide what you want. But I don't have to be part of it. I am resigning. Do you understand me?'

Paul could not speak.

'Do you understand me, Paul?'

'Yes,' he managed.

'If this colony goes back to the We, then it goes without me. I will not be guilty of that. Do you hear me? I will not be part of what you are doing. If you tell Earth, you lose me.

290

If you do it now, you lose me now. If you do it in the future, the same. Understand?'

With a horrible, hollow feeling Paul called up the communications menus. He looked at the last message out of the station. It was short and clear. It had been sent from May's workstation out over the laser less than half an hour before.

'It's gone, Lewis,' said Paul.

'*God!*' howled Lewis. 'You . . . shit!'

And beside him Paul heard May whisper, 'Paul!' as if she were in pain.

'God!' cried Lewis again.

And Paul pleaded, 'Lewis!'

I should have lied, he thought. But he had not dared to try.

'Lewis,' he said urgently. 'We can't do it all by ourselves—'

He stopped himself. Inbreeding. Madness. Starvation . . . Why should Lewis listen to any of that?

'Lewis,' he tried again. 'You know Earth already suspects—'

Again he stopped himself. Fearfully he called up the field readings.

'*God!*' Lewis was weeping.

The field readings had not changed.

'You've ruined it!' groaned Lewis. 'Our last chance. You've ruined it. Why? Why couldn't we at least wait to see if the child survived? Or if you and Van could—' He stopped.

Child, thought Paul. Yes, Lewis. Please think of your child. Please.

'Stupid,' said Lewis. 'To go like this.'

'Lewis – we need you!'

Silence.

Paul drew breath.

But what could he say? What could he possibly say to Lewis? What could have meaning to him now? He looked at the others. Erin had gone – vanished from behind him. Perhaps she had gone to pray. Perhaps that was the only hope now.

Beside him May was white-faced, watching the screen, which showed only the stillness of Thorsten's tomb.

'Lewis,' he said again. 'We need you.'

Silence.

He drew breath. But there was nothing more he could say. He had said everything now. There was nothing he could do, except wait.

And wait.

In silence.

And soon – or sometime – he would have to try to reach the crawler. He would have to ride out there, perched precariously on the back of one of the utilities. Taking it as slowly as he could. To reach the place and recover the crawler, whose airlock door would be open now. To do what he could for the body that would be lying on the ice beside it. So frozen that it would shatter at a touch.

Soon. He would have to do it soon – now, even, before all power was lost from the crawler.

And if anything went wrong, the station would be down to two.

Lewis, he thought. *We need you!*

Lewis groaned. 'Why don't we see stars here?' he said. And 'Shit.'

Silence.

'All right,' Lewis sighed. 'On one condition.'

'You're coming back?'

'You have to let me talk to Earth myself,' Lewis said. 'You don't try to lock me out of the comms. Ever.'

'I won't.'

The screen still showed the cairn where Thorsten lay. Nothing moved. The crawler was not moving either.

Paul said, 'What's your power reading?'

'Forty-two per cent. It'll be all right. Don't worry.'

'Are you coming back now?'

'In just a moment.'

'Do you want me to send up a crawler?'

293

'No. I'll be all right.'

There was a short pause. Then Lewis said, 'She might die, you know. We might lose her and the child. Then this would all be for nothing.'

Paul looked at May again. She shook her head slightly. She would not tell her man she could hear him. Not now.

'I don't think she'll die, Lewis,' said Paul, with his eyes on her.

'Thank you for that at least,' said Lewis.

Silence. Still no movement on the screen. He was looking at the landscape, thinking about death. About what he had nearly done. What he still might do.

'What have we said to Earth?' he asked.

Lewis!

But he must have remembered the Listener too, because he added, 'Careful.'

'You'll see when you come in,' said Paul.

'All right.'

'Are you coming down now?'

'Yes, I'm on my way. But you need to understand what I'm going to do, Paul. I'm going to confuse Earth. I'm going to send such nonsense that it'll think we're mad. It won't trust our findings. This is the last hope. You have to let me try. I won't stop you sending what you decide to send. But you must not stop me either.'

'I won't stop you,' promised Paul.

May's message had requested a translation program. Earth would send that now. They would want to double-check the data, look for patterns, study every blip that had occurred in the ten years of the station's history. Everything the creature was trying to hide about itself would now stream Sunward over the laser link. Nothing Lewis could do would change that. His last hope was hopeless.

Lewis was right about only one thing. They had been tired and scared. There had been nothing logical in the way they had thought about it. It had been the worst of all possible times to make their decision.

But that was how the mind worked. That was how it decided what 'we' meant, and that *now* was the moment to choose.

And love, morality, freedom and free will – none of those things had counted. In the end they had chosen to give the next generation the best chance. The genes had seen to that. Of course they had.

'Will he make it?' said May softly.

'Yes, I think so.'

'You nearly didn't.'

'He's a better driver. And I had drained the power further. I was using the crawler equipment, remember.'

He picked up the view from the crawler again. It was in

motion, tipping forward down the steep incline of the Highway. There in the valley bottom was the station, the scattered flare of the mirrors, the huge dull curves of the domes, the gleam of ice that flowed away from beneath it. In the light of Lewis's headlamps individual lumps crawled towards them and disappeared off the bottom or the sides of the screen.

May put her head in her hands.

'Are you all right?' he asked.

'Fine – just shattered. God, I'm so tired! And as soon as he's back we'll be into who can say what to Earth, and what the rules are and all that. And we'll have to live with it until he can get himself to accept what's happened. And I'm the one he'll blame most . . .' Her hair had fallen about her face. She pushed it back. It wavered in the air. 'Thanks, Paul. For a moment I thought we'd killed him there, between us. But you got him back. Thanks . . .'

'He came back for us.'

'Yeah. He does care about us. We all care, in the end. Even Van does.'

'Erin.'

'You think she'll let us call her that?'

'Things may be changing with her now.'

'That would be good.'

And she added, 'Well done, Paul.'

They watched the station grow nearer and nearer. Its outlines grew to the edge of the screen and were lost. Now Paul could see the occasional flicker of the particle action in the outer layer. He had time to watch for it, as he had never had before – the momentary little glow as a mote from space was absorbed within the station's first skin. Yesterday, during the bombardment, it must have been alive with light. The shadows of the ice-shapes would have danced and twisted like creatures in a cold hell. But there were no shadows now.

'Of course,' said Lewis suddenly, 'we don't know how long Earth will take to react. Does it think something like this through in days, or decades? It might all be pointless. We might all be dead by the time it makes up its mind.'

Paul thought that it had taken less than a year for Earth to decide to send him out here. But he remembered that other presence, listening. He said nothing.

'It would bugger things up for our descendants, though,' said Lewis. 'This generation or the next. It would come to the same thing in the end.'

The crawler was approaching the outer airlock. Paul did not wait for Lewis to open the door. He did it himself.

'Maybe we'll have grown strong enough to fight them off,' said Lewis.

Still Paul said nothing. When the outer door closed behind the crawler he let out a long, silent breath.

'I'm going to make it think we've gone mad,' said Lewis. 'Why not? I thought it was mad to start with and I live here! I'll make it think we're *trying* to get it to come . . .'

'Maybe,' said Paul warily. Even though Lewis was inside the station they were still using the radio link. A signal broadcast in the station might well leak out. And the Listener was still there.

They followed the crawler through the layers. Paul switched to the hangar view to see it arrive. They watched Lewis's suited figure appear, dock the power feed and meticulously complete the exterior checks before turning towards the living quarters. Only when he knew Lewis was in the living-quarter airlock, when he saw the pressure climbing back towards normal, did he at last switch the view.

He chose the land of the Hunter – the wavering yellow grasses, the hard blue sky. He projected it all around the common room, overriding the lighting and the ceiling display, so that all memories of outside were hidden and the whole of that large chamber was bright with the imaginary scene. It was huge and yet no detail was lost. On the horizon was a line of clouds – great thunderheads that would spill their fire and water in huge quantities over the virtual plain. He saw that Erin had been right, that their undersides were dark and feathery, and that they trailed dark diagonal streaks which were the falling sheets of rain. He had not noticed those before. Of the Hunter himself there was no sign.

And the message they had sent would still be on its way to its destination. Even if the laser had fired at once, the little pulses of energy that told the story would only now be approaching the orbit of the inner gas giants. They would still have an hour or more to fly before they reached the receptors on Earth. Yet they were travelling, and at the speed of light. Nothing could stop them or call them back. The future had already been chosen.

The airlock hatch opened and closed. Lewis was there, looking older and more tired than Paul had ever seen him.

'Sorry,' he said. 'I've been a fool.'

'You had us *shitting* ourselves!' said May fiercely. She took a long skip towards him. Her arm lifted as if to strike him. Lewis flinched. But at the last moment it went around the back of his neck and caught her other wrist there. She pushed her face into his chest.

'I'm *never* letting you go out again,' she said. 'Not without one of us to keep an eye on you.'

'Sorry,' he said again. His arm was around her waist.

Paul watched them clinging to each other by the airlock door. No one spoke. Behind them the grasses waved on the walls, yellow under the blue sky.

'What do you think?' said Lewis at last. 'Will Earth believe you?'

'Earth will believe us,' Paul said.

'What makes you so sure?'

'It knows there must be someone else.'

Afterwards he went to look for Erin.

Acknowledgements

This novel was drafted and the title chosen before my attention was drawn to Yevgeny Zamyatin's novel *We*, published in English in 1924. I have only my ignorance to blame, for Zamyatin's novel is an important forerunner of the dystopian genre, inspiring Orwell's *1984* and influencing many others.

I did look for another title (*Cold Eden* seemed a possibility, although this again was not original). But nothing else captures with such short, stark simplicity the theme I wanted to write about – the place of the individual in the larger group, which is of course the meat of all dystopian fiction. So *We* it remains. And now I too owe a debt to the great Russian.

I also want to thank the members of the Physics and Astronomy Department of the Open University – Nigel Mason, Sylvia Miller, Jon Dawson, Stephen Wolters and Aaron Gronstal – for their help with the scientific aspects of the novel, and all those many others who have read the typescript or otherwise contributed: Kim, Bruce, Amanda, Alan, Ginger, David, Hannah, both Alisons, Sophie and Dr Daryl Dobb – thank you all so very much.

John Dickinson